ECHOES OF LOVE

A SAGA OF SELF-DISCOVERY

SHANU CHANDRA

This work is humbly dedicated to the spiritual masters of Bharat, whose steadfast devotion and rigorous discipline have safeguarded the profound wisdom of human enlightenment for generations. It is through their efforts that this ancient knowledge reaches us in its most unadulterated form, a gift to humanity.

Contents

Preface

In moments of quiet reflection, I've delved into the complex interplay of light and shadow that shapes our existence. Though this book is a work of fiction, it draws from a deep, experiential journey through life's varied emotions, exploring their origins and their profound impact on our lives. It bridges the gap between our true selves and the external perceptions that often define us.

Becoming an author was not a path I consciously chose but rather one that unfolded from a deep-seated need to share the experiences that have profoundly influenced my understanding of self and society. This tale, while centering on a singular journey, resonates with a universal theme: the struggle with being misunderstood, misjudged, and feeling out of place.

It's a story about finding your voice, discovering your strength, and turning your dreams into reality. It's about showing that even those who feel overlooked or underestimated have the power to change their lives and the lives of others.

So, if you've ever felt out of place, undervalued, or simply different, this story is for you. It's a reminder that the path to finding yourself and achieving greatness doesn't always follow the conventional route.

Throughout this book, I've endeavored to impart a lesson at the end of each chapter, serving as a mirror to life's reflections. Additionally, I've highlighted key learnings in italics to draw attention to their importance. These insights are offered with the hope that they may enrich your wisdom and guide you on your journey.

Welcome to a journey of transformation, from the quiet shadows of doubt to the bright future of possibility.

Acknowledgements

Echoes of Love is a journey that has been shaped by the love, support, and inspiration of many incredible people, and I am deeply grateful for each of you.

To my family—thank you for being my rock, for believing in me when I doubted myself, and for always encouraging me to chase my dreams. Your unwavering support has been the foundation on which this book stands. To my parents, for your patience and guidance, and to my siblings, for being my first and forever cheerleaders—I owe you everything.

To my friends, who have shared in this journey with me—thank you for your understanding during late-night brainstorming sessions, for being the voices of reason when I felt lost in the whirlwind of writing, and for filling my life with joy and inspiration. Your encouragement has been a constant source of strength.

A special thanks to my mentors and teachers, whose wisdom and guidance have not only shaped this story but also shaped the person I've become. Your belief in my ability to create something meaningful gave me the courage to take that leap of faith.

To the characters of this novel, Rahul and Meera, thank you for letting me tell your story. You both hold a special place in my heart, and through you, I've discovered new depths of love, resilience, and transformation.

Finally, to my readers—this book is for you. Thank you for choosing to walk this path with me, for immersing yourselves in the world of Echoes of Love, and for embracing the emotions, struggles, and beauty within its pages. Your support means the world to me.

May the echoes of love in this story resonate in your hearts, and may you always find beauty in the love that surrounds you.

With heartfelt gratitude,
Shanu Chandra

Prologue

This book delves into the transformative years of youth-a pivotal time that lays the foundation for our future. It captures a phase filled with dreams, aspirations, and the quest for identity. Among the students who walk the college corridors, some shine brightly, earning the adoration of peers and the accolades of teachers. However, this narrative shifts the focus to those who linger in the shadows, the unsung individuals whose brilliance is not immediately visible.

These are the quiet dreamers, the thinkers, often misunderstood or overlooked:

Mistaken for arrogant when simply shy, Perceived as ignorant, yet deeply introverted, Seen as distant, though profoundly thoughtful, Labeled fearful for their caution, Misunderstood as aloof in their reflection,

Mistaken for snobbish in their selectivity of friends, Viewed as indecisive, yet they're patient,

Considered lacking ambition, when they find joy in simplicity, Judged impractical, though they're dreamers, Seen as complicated for their depth.

This story invites you to walk alongside Rahul, experiencing his trials and triumphs as reflections of your own.

"Echoes of love" is not merely about navigating the heart's complex landscape but about recognizing the broader journey of self-understanding and acceptance.

Join this voyage, where each page promises insight and inspiration, reminding us that the greatest adventures begin when we dare to look beyond. Welcome to "Echoes of love"-a journey where the true learning lies in the paths we carve for ourselves, beyond the confines of love.

ONE
THE BEGINNING

"Friendship is born at that moment when one person says to another,
'What I You too? I thought I was the only one."
- C.S. Lewis

Shantiniketan College was a world in itself. It sprawled across acres of land, dotted with ancient trees, open fields, and brick pathways. The grand, ivy-covered buildings stood as quiet witnesses to generations of students who had walked their corridors. For newcomers like Rahul, the campus felt endless—intimidating yet full of possibilities.

Rahul, with his shy demeanor and reserved personality, felt like a small drop in the vast ocean of students. He had always preferred the comfort of books to people. For someone like him, friendship didn't come naturally—it needed time, and trust. Yet, as he sat on a weathered bench beneath the banyan tree that dominated the college courtyard, he found himself watching the world unfold around him.

It was the first week of college, and the buzz of excitement hung in the air. Freshmen hurried past him, some looking as lost as Rahul felt. Seniors lounged in groups, casually claiming their territory in the open spaces. Rahul, book in hand, had chosen this spot for its quiet. He loved how the banyan tree's massive branches created a canopy, casting cool shadows on the ground.

In the early days, Rahul mostly kept to himself. His interactions were polite but minimal—he would nod at classmates, offer the occasional smile, but rarely did he join in the conversations that happened around him. His classes, though interesting, were overwhelming, not because of the workload but because of the people. They all seemed to know each other already, like they had formed invisible circles of friends that Rahul couldn't step into.

But, like all new experiences, things slowly began to change.

One day, after a particularly long class, Rahul found himself sitting alone in the campus cafeteria. His tray held a simple lunch—rice, dal, and a vegetable curry. He was poking at his food absentmindedly, lost in thought, when a voice interrupted him.

"Mind if I sit here?"

Rahul looked up to see a tall boy with a wide smile and messy hair. It was Sameer, a classmate he had seen in a few lectures but never spoken to. Before Rahul could answer, Sameer had already pulled out a chair and plopped down across from him.

"I'm Sameer," he introduced himself, offering his hand. "I've seen you in class. Rahul, right?"

Rahul nodded, shaking his hand with a slight hesitation. "Yeah, that's me."

From that moment, Sameer seemed to decide that Rahul was going to be his friend. Sameer was everything Rahul wasn't—outgoing, loud, and always cracking jokes. He had an easy charm about him that made people gravitate toward him. Over the next few days, Sameer started dragging Rahul into conversations, introducing him to other classmates, and even convincing him to join group lunches.

At first, Rahul found it overwhelming. The group Sameer hung out with was big, and everyone had strong personalities. But gradually, Rahul realized that the more time he spent with them, the more comfortable he felt. They laughed about silly things, made fun of their professors, and bonded over shared struggles with assignments. The cafeteria became their meeting spot, and soon Rahul found himself looking forward to these daily interactions.

The first year of college unfolded with all the joy and chaos of newfound independence. Days were a blur of classes, group projects, and the occasional bunked lecture. Rahul, despite his reserved nature, found himself being pulled into the social fabric of college life.

It was during one of these lunches that Rahul met Meera properly. She was sitting at the far end of the table, laughing with a few of the girls in their group. Rahul had seen her around before, but they had never spoken much. She had a presence that was hard to miss—her energy, her smile, her laughter that seemed to brighten even the dullest afternoons.

"Rahul," Sameer called out, motioning toward Meera. "Have you met Meera?"

Rahul shook his head, feeling a little self-conscious. Meera turned toward him and smiled—a warm, easy smile that reached her eyes.

"Hey," she said, waving slightly. "I've seen you around."

"Yeah, we share a couple of classes," Rahul replied, his voice barely above a whisper.

From that point, Rahul and Meera began to cross paths more frequently. At first, it was just in passing—quick exchanges of smiles or waves as they moved between classes. But soon, those brief moments turned into longer conversations. Meera was easy to talk to, even for someone as shy as Rahul. She had a way of making people feel comfortable, of drawing them out of their shells without even trying.

Life at Shantiniketan was more than just classes. It was the little moments between lectures—the shared cups of tea at the campus canteen, the rushed walks to make it to the next class on time, and the endless conversations that started as jokes and somehow turned into deep, philosophical debates.

Rahul's group of friends quickly became his support system. They studied together, laughed together, and even shared meals. Sameer, with his easygoing nature, often took charge, organizing impromptu cricket matches or movie nights in the dorms. Rahul wasn't one for sports, but he joined in, happy to be part of something bigger than himself.

There was also Ankit, the quiet one of the group, who, like Rahul, preferred books to people. Then there was Priya, whose sarcastic remarks and dry humor kept everyone on their toes. And finally, there was Meera—who somehow managed to be the glue that held them all together.

Meera started cooking lunch for the group at times. She would bring homemade food packed in small tiffin boxes and insist that everyone share. Rahul, who was still adjusting to life away from home, found comfort in the warmth of her food and her kindness. They would sit together on the grass, laughing and talking, passing food around as the sun filtered through the trees.

With each passing day, Rahul felt himself growing closer to Meera. It wasn't anything dramatic—there was no grand declaration of feelings, no sudden realization. It was in the small things—the way she remembered that he liked his tea without sugar, the way she teased him about his love for old books, the way they could sit in comfortable silence without needing to fill the gaps with words.

One afternoon, as they sat together under the banyan tree, Meera asked him about his plans for the future.

"What do you want to do after college?" she asked, her head resting on her knees as she looked at him with curiosity.

Rahul shrugged, unsure how to put his dreams into words. "I don't know. I guess... I'd like to write. Maybe novels or short stories. Something like that."

Meera smiled, her eyes lighting up. "You'd be great at that. I can already imagine you as this famous author, sitting in some cozy house by the sea, typing away."

Rahul chuckled, the idea both thrilling and terrifying. "What about you?"

"Journalism," Meera said with conviction. "I want to write stories that matter. Things that change people's perspectives, you know?"

They spent the rest of the afternoon talking about their dreams, their fears, and everything in between. It was in these conversations that their bond deepened—no longer just acquaintances or friends, but something more.

College life was full of fun moments—late-night study sessions that often turned into midnight snack runs, impromptu dance parties in someone's dorm room, or lazy Sundays spent lounging around campus with no real plans. Rahul's group became his family away from home. They were always there for each other—whether it was to help with a tough assignment or to celebrate someone's birthday with cake and laughter.

One weekend, they all decided to head to the lake just outside the college grounds. It was a quiet spot, surrounded by trees, with clear water that reflected the sky. They spent the day playing games, lounging by the water, and just enjoying the peace away from the busy college life. Rahul found himself sitting next to Meera as they watched the others splashing around in the lake, laughing and shouting.

"I'm glad we're friends," Meera said quietly, her voice soft but sincere.

"Me too," Rahul replied, his heart swelling with warmth. It was in that moment that he realized just how much she had come to mean to him.

As the first year of college drew to a close, Rahul found himself reflecting on how much had changed. He had started the year as a shy, unsure boy, keeping to himself and avoiding large groups. But now, he was surrounded by friends, each of whom had made his college experience richer and more meaningful.

And then there was Meera—the girl who had somehow become his closest confidante, his partner in both laughter and silence. Their friendship was easy, natural, and yet, Rahul couldn't help but wonder if there was something more beneath the surface.

As he looked ahead to the rest of his college journey, Rahul felt a sense of excitement and nervousness. The future was uncertain, but for the first time in his life, he wasn't facing it alone.

By building on Rahul's shy nature, his gradual immersion into college life, and the deepening bond with his friends and Meera, we create a rich, layered narrative. The daily life scenes—meals together, campus moments, and the shared experiences—will bring vibrancy to this chapter. Each scene contributes to Rahul's development, setting the stage for the challenges and growth that will follow in later chapters.

The sun hovered like a golden orb above the sprawling campus of Shantiniketan College, casting long shadows on the paths that wound through the lush greenery. Its rays filtered through the tall trees that lined the courtyard, creating patterns of light and shadow on the ground. It was late afternoon, and the college buzzed with activity. Freshmen hurried to and fro, their excitement and anxiety palpable, as they navigated the unfamiliar territory. The seniors, however, moved at a more leisurely pace, basking in the knowledge that they had already conquered this place, or so they liked to think.

Rahul sat on a weathered wooden bench beneath the shade of an ancient banyan tree, the heart of the campus, a favorite spot for students to gather. It was here, under the banyan's massive, twisting branches, that many friendships had been formed, secrets shared, and hearts broken. Rahul had chosen this spot for its solitude, away from the hustle of students moving between classes. A gentle breeze rustled the leaves overhead, bringing with it the faint scent of jasmine from the nearby gardens.

In his hands, Rahul held a well-worn copy of a classic novel, its pages dog-eared from countless readings. He had always loved books, finding in them a world far more predictable and controllable than the one he inhabited. He traced the edges of the book absentmindedly, lost in thought. His final year of college loomed on the horizon, a year that promised both freedom and uncertainty. What awaited him after this, he wondered? The idea of graduating, stepping into the real world, left him feeling both excited and terrified.

He was still mulling over these thoughts when he heard it—her laughter. It was a sound that carried across the quad like music, distinct and vibrant. He didn't have to look up to know who it was. Meera. She had that effect on people; her presence was like a magnet, drawing everyone to her without even trying. Her laughter was infectious, the kind that made you smile even if you didn't know the joke.

Rahul glanced up just as Meera appeared in his line of sight, her long, flowing hair catching the golden light of the setting sun. She was surrounded by a small group of friends, but her energy seemed to radiate beyond them. Her face, always alive with expression, was lit up by a bright, easy smile, the kind that could make even the most stressful day seem trivial. She was wearing a simple yet elegant kurti, the fabric swaying with her every step, and as she approached, her eyes scanned the courtyard, landing on him.

Their eyes met, and for a brief moment, time seemed to slow down. Rahul felt a jolt, an electric connection that sparked between them, as if the universe had paused to acknowledge their encounter. Meera's gaze lingered for just a second longer than necessary before she broke into a wide grin, walking directly toward him.

"Is that Shakespeare you're hiding?" she teased, her voice full of playful mischief as she plopped down beside him on the bench without waiting for an invitation.

Rahul smirked, sliding the book into his lap. "Maybe. Or maybe I'm just trying to impress a certain someone."

Meera rolled her eyes, but the light blush that crept onto her cheeks betrayed her. She punched him lightly on the shoulder, the familiarity of their banter as natural as the leaves rustling above them. From that moment, something shifted between them—an unspoken connection that was more than just casual friendship. It was the beginning of something new, something neither of them could have predicted.

The weeks that followed were a blur of shared moments. Rahul and Meera, once casual acquaintances, quickly became inseparable. It started with simple conversations in between classes, but soon those brief moments turned into long hours spent together. They found themselves drawn to the same corners of the campus, seeking out quiet places where they could talk freely, uninterrupted by the bustle of college life.

They frequented the campus library, an old, brick building with tall arched windows that let in streams of sunlight during the day and cast long shadows in the evening. It was here that they shared countless late-night study sessions, surrounded by the musty scent of old books and the faint aroma of coffee that always seemed to linger. The quiet hum of the library, punctuated only by the soft rustling of pages, became the backdrop for their conversations.

"I think you'd make a great journalist," Rahul said one evening, looking up from his notes. Meera had just finished explaining her passion for writing, her desire to chase stories and uncover truths that would otherwise remain hidden.

"You think so?" she asked, her eyes lighting up at the compliment. Journalism had always been her dream, but hearing someone else believe in her made it feel more real.

"Absolutely," he replied with conviction. "You have this energy, this way of seeing the world that not everyone has. People would listen to you."

Meera smiled, a genuine, heartfelt smile that made Rahul's chest tighten. "And you?" she asked, her voice softer now. "What about you and your novels? I can already picture your name on the cover of a bestseller."

Rahul chuckled, though there was a hint of seriousness in his tone. "That's the dream. Writing novels, traveling the world, living in a little house by the sea, and just...writing." He leaned back in his chair, his gaze drifting to the window where the sun was beginning to set, painting the sky in hues of orange and pink.

Together, they painted a picture of a future that felt limitless. They envisioned lives filled with creativity and adventure, where they would both chase their dreams, side by side. Their connection deepened with each passing day, not just through their shared goals, but through the small, intimate moments they created together.

They discovered hidden corners of the campus that few knew about—a secluded spot by the lake where they often sat in silence, watching the ripples of water dance in the sunlight, or a tiny café just outside the campus gates where they would sneak away between classes for a stolen moment of peace. Their laughter became a soundtrack to their shared experiences, echoing in the quiet hallways and across the open fields. They were no longer just friends. They were partners—partners in every sense of the word.

As their junior year drew to a close, the excitement and apprehension of their final year began to loom over them. There was a sense of finality in the air, as if time was running out. They made promises to each other, vows that they would support one another through the challenges ahead—exams, assignments, job applications, everything that their final year would throw at them.

"No matter what happens, we'll face it together," Meera said one evening, her voice filled with determination as they stood by the lake, the moonlight reflecting off the water.

Rahul nodded, squeezing her hand. "Together," he agreed, his heart swelling with a mixture of hope and fear. He wanted to believe that they could conquer anything, but there was a small, nagging doubt that lingered in the back of his mind. Life, he knew, had a way of throwing curveballs when you least expected them.

That summer, life threw its first curveball.

Meera, who had always been the vibrant, energetic force in Rahul's life, began to feel unwell. At first, it was nothing serious—just a bit of fatigue, something easily brushed aside in the whirlwind of college life. But as the weeks wore on, her symptoms worsened. She became more tired, more irritable, struggling to keep up with her studies. Rahul noticed the change almost immediately, though he didn't say anything at first, hoping it was just a passing phase.

"You don't look well, Meera," he finally said one evening, as they sat on the steps of the library, the sky painted in soft shades of pink and orange as the sun set behind them.

"I'm fine," she replied, forcing a smile. "Just a little tired."

But Rahul wasn't convinced. He could see the toll it was taking on her, both physically and emotionally. Her once boundless energy was gone, replaced by a weariness that she couldn't hide. And though she tried to put on a brave face, Rahul could see the fear in her eyes.

"Maybe you should see a doctor," he suggested gently, but Meera shook her head.

"I'm fine, Rahul. Really. It's nothing."

But as summer turned to autumn, and autumn to winter, it became clear that it wasn't nothing. Meera's condition worsened. She missed classes more frequently, her grades began to slip, and the vibrant girl Rahul had fallen in love with seemed to be fading before his eyes.

Her parents, who had always been protective of her, grew increasingly concerned. They scheduled a visit to see her, and Rahul could sense the growing tension between them. They didn't want to believe that their daughter's struggles were just a result of the pressures of college life. They needed someone to blame, and Rahul feared they were beginning to see him as the reason for her decline.

One chilly evening, after a particularly difficult day of classes, Meera broke down in Rahul's arms. "What if I can't get better?" she whispered, her voice trembling with fear. "What if this affects everything? My future...our future?"

Rahul held her tightly, his heart breaking at the sight of her so vulnerable. "You will get better, Meera," he whispered fiercely. "We'll get through this together. I promise."

But as the final year approached, with all its pressures and expectations, Rahul couldn't shake the feeling of dread that settled over him. The dream of a future they had envisioned together felt more fragile with each passing day. He wanted to believe that their love was strong enough to withstand anything, but life, he knew, had a way of testing even the strongest of bonds.

In the heart of Shantiniketan College, amidst the laughter, the dreams, and the memories they had created, shadows began to creep in. Neither Rahul nor Meera could have predicted the storm that was coming, a storm that would test the very foundation of their relationship.

ᗺᗺᗺ

"Each fresh start brings a surge of energy and the opportunity to accomplish what we haven't yet achieved, inviting us to explore, learn, and transform with every step we take."

TWO
SHADOW OF
ILLNESS

"Attraction is the temporary love, but love is the permanent attraction."
- Sri Sri Ravi Shankar

The final semester at Shantiniketan College had arrived, and with it came the sense that everything was changing. The sprawling campus, usually so full of life, felt quieter, as if the trees and paths themselves were holding their breath, waiting for what was to come. Rahul had always found solace in the familiar rhythm of the college—the early morning rush, the chatter between classes, the late-night study sessions—but now, everything felt different. And it wasn't just the impending end of college life that weighed on him; it was Meera.

Meera's energy, the spark that had once lit up every corner of his world, was dimming. At first, Rahul told himself it was just the stress of exams and the constant pressure of the final semester. But soon, the signs became impossible to ignore. Meera was no longer the vibrant, carefree girl who had captured his heart. Her laugh, once so full of life, had become a rare sound. Her eyes, once bright with curiosity and mischief, now looked tired, burdened by something unseen.

In the early days of their relationship, Rahul had admired Meera's resilience—how she balanced her ambitions, her friendships, and her love for him with an effortless grace. But now, that grace seemed to be slipping away, leaving behind a girl who was battling something far more serious than exam stress.

One afternoon, they sat together beneath the old banyan tree on campus, their usual meeting spot since the early days of their friendship. The breeze carried the faint scent of jasmine, and students passed by in groups, laughing and chatting about weekend plans. But here, in their small corner of the world, everything was still.

"Rahul," Meera said softly, her voice barely above a whisper.

He looked up from the book he was pretending to read, sensing the heaviness in her tone. "What is it?"

"I don't feel like myself anymore," she admitted, her eyes downcast, fingers nervously tracing the edges of her notebook. "I'm tired all the time. I don't know what's happening."

Rahul's heart tightened. He had noticed her weariness, the way she struggled to keep up with her classes, how her once-vibrant personality had dulled. He reached out, taking her hand in his. "We'll figure it out, Meera. You're just going through a rough patch. It'll get better."

But even as he said the words, he wasn't sure he believed them. Deep down, Rahul felt an unsettling fear growing. There was something more to this than just stress, but neither of them wanted to say it aloud.

They spent the rest of that day in silence, sitting together under the banyan tree, the unspoken tension between them hanging in the air.

Over the following weeks, Rahul and Meera's relationship became both their solace and their burden. Rahul found himself clinging to every moment they spent together, desperate to make her smile again, to see her laugh like she used to. They spent more time alone, retreating to the quiet corners of the campus that had become their sanctuary—by the lake, in the old library, or in the small café just outside the college gates.

The café had become a ritual for them. Every day, after lunch, they would escape the bustling campus to sit in the dimly lit booth at the back of the café, where the smell of freshly brewed coffee and the sound of soft music offered a brief respite from the pressures of college life.

"You remember our first year?" Meera asked one day, a wistful smile playing on her lips. "How we barely knew each other, and now look at us."

Rahul smiled, the memory flooding back. He had been so shy back then, keeping to himself, lost in his books. It was Meera who had drawn him out of his shell. She had seen something in him that no one else had—the quiet depth, the thoughtful mind behind the reserved exterior. Slowly, she had become his closest friend, and eventually, something more.

"I was terrified of you," Rahul admitted, his eyes twinkling with mischief.

Meera laughed, a soft sound that sent warmth through Rahul's chest. "You were terrified of every girl."

"True," he said, leaning back in his chair, his eyes locked on hers. "But you were different."

A brief silence settled between them, one filled with the weight of their shared memories. Rahul felt the pull of nostalgia—how easy things had been back then, how simple their connection had seemed. Now, everything felt so much more complicated.

As the days passed, Rahul couldn't shake the feeling that something was terribly wrong. Meera's health continued to decline, and though she tried to hide it, he could see the fear in her eyes. She wasn't just tired—she was weakening, and it terrified him.

One evening, after a particularly exhausting day of classes, Rahul found Meera sitting by the lake, her shoulders hunched, her face pale in the fading light. He sat down beside her, wrapping his arm around her shoulders.

"Meera, you need to see a doctor," he said gently, though there was an edge of desperation in his voice.

She shook her head. "I'm fine, Rahul. I don't want to make a big deal out of this."

"It is a big deal," Rahul insisted. "You're not okay, and I'm scared. We need to figure out what's going on."

Meera looked at him then, her eyes filled with unshed tears. "What if it's something serious? What if...I'm not the same person anymore? What if I can't handle it?"

Rahul's heart ached as he pulled her closer. "Whatever it is, we'll face it together. I love you, Meera. Nothing's going to change that."

For a moment, the world seemed to slow down. The lake shimmered in the fading sunlight, and the only sound was the soft rustling of leaves in the breeze. Meera leaned into Rahul, her head resting on his shoulder. It was one of those rare moments when words weren't necessary, when the silence between them said more than anything else could.

But even in that moment of peace, Rahul couldn't ignore the gnawing fear that lingered at the edges of his mind. Something was wrong, and no amount of love could stop the storm that was coming.

As Meera's condition worsened, her parents became more involved, and their relationship with Rahul grew increasingly strained. Meera's father, a stern man who had always been protective of his daughter, began to view Rahul as a distraction—a boy who had led Meera down a path of stress and overwork.

"He's not good for you, Meera," her father said one evening when she was visiting home. "You need to focus on your health. This boy...he's a distraction you can't afford right now."

Meera's protests fell on deaf ears. Her parents, though well-meaning, couldn't understand the depth of her connection with Rahul. They saw him as a complication, a reason for her deteriorating health, rather than the source of comfort he had become.

The conflict between them escalated, creating a rift in Meera's life. She was caught between the two people she loved most—her parents, who had always protected her, and Rahul, who had become her anchor in the storm.

As the semester wore on, Rahul found himself more isolated than ever. His friends had started to notice his absence, the way he had withdrawn into himself, consumed by his concern for Meera. They tried to reach out, to pull him back into the fold of their daily college life, but Rahul's thoughts were always with Meera.

One afternoon, he sat with a group of friends in the courtyard, their usual banter flowing around him, but he felt distant, disconnected. His best friend, Amit, nudged him. "Rahul, you've been awfully quiet lately. Everything okay?"

Rahul forced a smile. "Yeah, just...a lot on my mind."

Amit gave him a knowing look but didn't push. They all knew about Meera's condition, though no one spoke about it openly. There was an unspoken understanding that Rahul was dealing with something heavy, something they couldn't quite grasp.

The tension in Rahul's life built to a breaking point one evening when Meera called him, her voice shaky and strained. "Rahul, I need to see you. Now."

Without hesitation, Rahul rushed to the lake, where Meera was waiting. She looked fragile, her usual confidence shattered. "What's wrong?" he asked, panic rising in his chest.

"My parents...they don't want me to see you anymore," Meera said, her voice breaking. "They think you're the reason I'm like this."

Rahul felt as if the ground had been pulled out from under him. "That's not true, Meera. You know that."

"I know," she whispered, tears streaming down her face. "But they don't. They're scared, Rahul. And I'm scared too."

Rahul pulled her into his arms, holding her tightly. "We'll figure this out, Meera. I won't let them take you away from me."

But even as he said the words, Rahul knew the situation was spiraling out of control. The love they had fought so hard to build was being tested in ways neither of them had expected, and the shadows that had crept into their lives were only growing dark.

ᐳᐳᐳ

"Genuine relationships evolve beyond initial physical attraction into deep connections rooted in compatibility, mutual respect, and shared experiences, transforming fleeting moments into lasting bond."

THREE

THE CONFRONTATION

"Change is the only permanent thing in life; it must be adopted gracefully. "
- Anonymous

The golden hues of the evening sun bathed the campus in a surreal, tranquil light as Rahul exited the library, his steps heavy with the burden of thoughts that had been haunting him for weeks. The pages of his textbooks felt alien in his hands, like tools of a forgotten life, as his mind wandered to a single focus: Meera. His heart ached with the memory of her—the girl whose laughter had once lit up the corners of Shantiniketan, now wilting like a flower starved of sunlight.

Their journey together had begun with the vibrancy of college life, where youthful dreams and shared ambitions painted their future. Late-night library sessions, study marathons fueled by coffee and dreams of top placements, had once been the norm. But now, as their final semester approached, those dreams felt distant—replaced by a shadow that neither of them had anticipated: Meera's health was failing.

Rahul had always admired Meera's resilience. She was a powerhouse of energy, balancing her academics, extracurriculars, and their relationship with grace. She had talked about becoming a successful corporate leader, envisioning herself in boardrooms, making decisions that shaped industries. But recently, that drive seemed to flicker like a candle on the verge of being extinguished.

He remembered one particular evening not long ago when they sat under the banyan tree by the sports ground. Meera had rested her head on his shoulder, the exhaustion clear in the slump of her frame. She had confided in him, her voice soft and laced with uncertainty, "Sometimes, I wonder if I'm losing sight of everything we worked for. I can't even focus on my projects anymore. My body feels like it's betraying me."

Rahul had brushed her hair aside gently, kissed her forehead, and whispered, "You're not alone in this, Meera. We'll get through it together. Once exams are over, we'll figure everything out."

But that promise seemed fragile now, like words uttered in a dream.

As Rahul approached the parking lot, the serene campus felt oddly quiet. The usual noise of students rushing from one class to another, their laughter and banter, was subdued. It was as though the world was holding its breath, sensing the storm about to descend upon him.

Suddenly, a voice shattered the stillness.

"There you are!"

The sharp tone cut through the air, startling Rahul from his reverie. He turned to see Meera's father standing a few feet away, his face contorted with anger. Flanking him were two police officers, their expressions stern.

A deep sense of foreboding tightened Rahul's chest. He had never seen Meera's father like this before, a man usually reserved, now brimming with rage. Rahul's heart sank as he realized this was more than just concern. This was an accusation.

"Sir, I was just leaving," Rahul said, trying to keep his voice calm, though he could feel his pulse quickening.

Meera's father stepped forward, his eyes narrowing with suspicion. His voice was low, laced with venom. "My daughter is suffering, and I hold you responsible."

Rahul blinked in disbelief. "Sir, I love Meera. I would never do anything to hurt her. I'm just trying to help her."

"You think this is help?" Her father's voice rose, cracking with fury. "She was fine until you came into her life. Focused, ambitious, full of life. And now look at her! She's sick, drained... and it's all because of you!"

The accusation hit Rahul like a blow. Meera's declining health was something he had tried desperately to manage, to understand, and now to be blamed for it—it felt like a nightmare.

As Rahul attempted to defend himself, one of the officers stepped closer. The tension in the air thickened, and before he could fully comprehend what was happening, they shoved him roughly against the stone wall. The scrape of the stone against his back felt real, searing, but it was the emotional pain that burned hotter.

Memories of their time together flashed before his eyes—the way Meera's face lit up whenever they talked about their future, the late-night strolls through campus, their whispered conversations about dreams and ambitions. And now, all of it was crumbling under the weight of accusations and misunderstandings.

Rahul's mind drifted back to a recent conversation they had, one evening at a quiet café near campus. Meera had spoken of her dreams with a wistful tone, "Rahul, do you think I'll ever make it? Be the woman I always wanted to be—strong, independent, changing the world?" Her question had been more of a plea, her eyes searching his for validation.

He had reached for her hand, his thumb tracing small circles on her wrist. "You're already that woman, Meera. You inspire everyone around you. And no matter what happens, we'll figure it out together."

They had laughed then, lost in their bubble of love, imagining their future together—careers flourishing, traveling the world, perhaps starting a life far from the chaos of their present. But now, as the cold stone bit into his back, that future seemed distant, if not impossible.

As the physical confrontation escalated, Rahul couldn't help but think of the impact this would have on their careers. Both of them had worked tirelessly to secure internships at top firms. Their future in the corporate world, the foundation of which had been laid through years of hard work, now seemed to be crumbling alongside their relationship.

Meera's parents had once praised Rahul's work ethic, admired his discipline and ambition. But now, in the heat of their misplaced anger, they were blinded by fear. Fear for their daughter, fear for her health, and a growing suspicion that Rahul's influence was the root cause of her suffering.

As the officers shoved him to the ground, Rahul's thoughts turned to Meera. How would she react to this? Would she be able to stand up to her parents? Or would this confrontation drive an irreparable wedge between them?

As Rahul lay on the cold pavement, pain radiating through his body, a quote echoed in his mind—something Meera had once shared with him: "The heart, like a mirror, reflects only that which it holds."

He had held love for Meera in his heart, unwavering and pure, but now, standing in the wreckage of their relationship, he wondered if that love was enough. Could they survive this storm? Could love truly conquer the doubt, fear, and anger that now surrounded them?

As Meera's father and the officers turned and walked away, Rahul's body trembled with exhaustion, his breath shallow and uneven. The place that had once been a sanctuary of knowledge and dreams now felt like a battleground.

Tears welled in his eyes as he forced himself to stand. The ache in his chest was far more unbearable than the bruises on his skin. He had fought for their love, for their shared future, but now everything seemed uncertain.

And as the sun dipped behind the horizon, casting long shadows over the campus, Rahul was left with the haunting realization that the real battle had only just begun.

♡♡♡

"Caring for our external selves complements inner beauty, as our body's well-being affects our mental and emotional states. Self-care is an act of self-respect, essential for a harmonious, confident, and fulfilled life."

"Self-expression is crucial in nurturing relationships and beyond. The absence of expression triggers a vicious cycle, with each missed opportunity introducing another layer of anxiety over potential reactions or the fear of being misunderstood."

FOUR
WHISHPERS OF FATE

There are moments in life when the winds of fate blow with such force that they seem to bend reality itself, altering the course of our lives forever."

The aftermath of the confrontation weighed heavily on Rahul. Each bruise on his body, each sharp pang of pain, was a reminder of the violence he had endured. But the emotional scars, those invisible cuts on his heart, were deeper and more lasting. What had once been a love story filled with laughter and shared dreams had now become a battlefield marked by fear, betrayal, and an overwhelming sense of loss.

As Rahul sat on the edge of his bed in his college dorm, he found himself trapped in a void of disbelief. Memories of his life with Meera flooded his mind—late-night phone calls, secret glances shared across crowded lecture halls, stolen moments under the stars. Now, those memories seemed distant, as if they belonged to someone else.

The weight of everything was too much to bear. He knew he needed to step away. Returning home to Bihar felt like his only escape, a refuge from the storm that had consumed his life in Shantiniketan. But he also knew that retreating would mean leaving behind the hopes and dreams they had built together.

The journey back to Bihar was a stark contrast to the tumultuous emotions swirling within him. The gentle sway of the train offered little comfort, as Rahul stared out of the window, watching the sprawling green fields and small villages roll by. Each passing station felt like a marker, counting down the distance between him and the life he had once known.

Back in Chapter 1, when Rahul had first arrived at Shantiniketan, he had been full of hope and excitement, determined to make the most of his time at the prestigious college. Meeting Meera had only deepened that sense of purpose. Together, they had dreamed of careers that would take them to the top of the corporate world, where they could shape industries and make a difference. But now, all of those dreams felt like they were slipping away, carried on the wind like whispers of fate.

When Rahul finally arrived at his family's home in Bihar, he was greeted with warmth and concern. His mother enveloped him in a tight embrace, her eyes brimming with questions she dared not ask. His father, ever the stoic, remained at a distance, watching his son with a quiet intensity, knowing that something had profoundly changed in him.

"Are you okay, beta?" his mother's voice was soft, filled with love but edged with anxiety.

Rahul forced a smile. "Just tired, Mom. That's all."

The lie hung heavy in the air, but his parents didn't push. They knew their son needed time. Rahul's father, a man of few words but immense strength, silently observed his son's struggle. He could see the torment Rahul was trying to hide, and though he didn't press for answers, he resolved to be there when his son was ready to open up.

In the quiet of his childhood room, Rahul found some semblance of comfort. The familiar scent of home, the old posters on the walls, and the distant sound of village life outside the window felt like a balm on his soul. But the pain, both physical and emotional, was still there, lurking just beneath the surface.

Rahul's mind wandered back to those early days with Meera. In Chapter 1, when they had first met, it had been during a heated debate in class. Meera's intelligence and passion had drawn him in immediately. She was fiercely ambitious, her dreams mirroring his own in many ways. They had bonded over long conversations about their futures, their shared desire to rise above their circumstances and make a mark on the world.

By Chapter 2, their relationship had deepened, moving from friendship to love. They had become each other's support system, their connection strengthened by shared goals and a mutual understanding of the pressures they faced. Meera had confided in Rahul about her family's expectations, the weight she felt to succeed not just for herself but for them as well. Rahul, in turn, had shared his own fears and insecurities about making it in a competitive world.

But now, in Chapter 3, all of that felt distant. The love that had once brought them together had been eclipsed by the harsh realities of life, and Rahul wasn't sure if it could ever be the same.

Rahul's thoughts also turned to his friends at Shantiniketan. In the midst of his turmoil with Meera, his friends had been his anchor, offering support and guidance. Anuj, his closest friend, had been there through it all, constantly pushing Rahul to stay focused on his studies, even as the situation with Meera's parents worsened. Anuj, too, had his own struggles—balancing his academic life with the pressure of securing a top internship, all while dealing with family expectations back home.

In an attempt to distract himself from his personal pain, Rahul had often helped Anuj prepare for interviews, their conversations shifting from personal matters to discussions about the corporate world, market trends, and business strategies. But even those moments of reprieve were short-lived. The weight of Meera's absence and the looming confrontation with her family always dragged him back to reality.

As May approached, and with it, the final exams, Rahul's anxiety grew. The prospect of returning to Shantiniketan filled him with dread. He wasn't sure if he could face Meera's family again, or even Meera herself. Her parents' threats echoed in his mind, and the memory of that brutal confrontation left him shaken.

It was during one of these low moments that Rahul's father stepped in. Observing his son's distress, he knew it was time to intervene.

"Rahul," his father said one evening, his voice calm and steady, "I know you're going through something difficult, but you can't let fear control your future. You've worked hard for this, and you deserve to finish what you started."

Those words struck a chord deep within Rahul. His father had always been a man of quiet strength, never one to give long speeches or emotional outbursts, but his words carried weight. They were rooted in experience, in the hardships he had faced in his own life. Rahul had always admired his father's ability to weather storms with a steady hand, and now, more than ever, he needed that strength.

With his father's support, Rahul began to find the courage to face his challenges. Together, they devised a plan. His father would accompany him back to Shantiniketan, offering moral support and standing by him if any further confrontations arose with Meera's family. The decision marked a turning point for Rahul. It wasn't just about finishing his exams—it was about reclaiming his life, his dreams, and his future.

The days leading up to their departure were filled with preparation. Rahul and his father spent hours going over notes, discussing strategies for the exams, and slowly, the atmosphere in their home shifted from one of despair to one of determination.

As Rahul packed his bags, he couldn't help but think about Meera. What was she doing now? Had she recovered from her illness? Were her parents still controlling every aspect of her life? He thought about the career they had both once dreamed of—working in the corporate world, making a difference, climbing the ladder of success together.

But now, their paths seemed to be diverging. Meera's illness and the pressures from her family had pulled her away from their shared vision. Rahul knew that his own career aspirations couldn't be put on hold forever, but he also couldn't ignore the love he still felt for her.

On the night before they were set to return to Shantiniketan, Rahul stood alone in the backyard of his family's home, staring up at the night sky. The stars, once a symbol of his and Meera's shared dreams, now seemed distant and cold. He wondered what the future held for them. Would they find their way back to each other? Or had fate already whispered its final verdict?

"Sometimes," his father had once told him, "life doesn't give us clear answers. We have to walk the path, even when we can't see where it leads."

And so, with a heart still heavy but a new resolve taking root, Rahul prepared to face whatever awaited him at Shantiniketan.

For in the end, the whispers of fate were not a sentence, but a challenge—to fight for what he believed in, to face his fears, and to hold onto hope, no matter how uncertain the future seemed.

This chapter, Whispers of Fate, ties back to the previous two chapters, weaving in the themes of love, career ambition, and family. It explores Rahul's internal struggle, his relationship with his father, and the way his love for Meera has been tested. The added scenes with Rahul's family and friends enrich the narrative, providing a deeper context for his emotional journey.

ᐅᐅᐅ

"Rejection, while painful, ignites self-discovery and growth, teaching us that our worth is defined not by others' acceptance but by our resilience and journey to self-worth."

FIVE
RESTORING HOPE

"Growth and comfort do not coexist."
Ginni Rometty

Months slipped by like grains of sand, each day blending seamlessly into the next as Rahul settled into a new routine in Bihar. The vibrant chaos of college life had given way to the quietude of his family home, where the only sounds were the gentle rustling of leaves and the distant calls of birds. Though he had faced his fears and successfully completed his exams, the absence of Meera left a gaping void in his heart. It was as if he had been living in shades of gray, missing the vibrant colors that she had once painted his world with.

The memories of their time together haunted him like restless ghosts—shared laughter that danced through the air, whispered dreams under the stars, and tender moments that felt etched into his very soul. Each recollection was a bittersweet reminder of what he had lost, and despite the distance and hurt, the bond they had forged during their years together refused to fade completely. It lingered, a thread woven into the fabric of his being, refusing to unravel despite the turmoil that had transpired.

One quiet evening, as Rahul scrolled through his phone, a message notification broke the heavy silence. His heart raced as he saw the name flash across the screen: Meera. An unexpected rush of emotions flooded through him, igniting a mix of excitement and anxiety. With trembling fingers, he opened the message, his pulse quickening at the weight of the words he read.

"Hey, Rahul. I hope you're doing okay. I've been thinking about you."

Those simple words carried the weight of their shared history, and in that moment, a flicker of hope ignited within him. It was as if the universe had conspired to bring them back together, a gentle reminder that love does not easily fade. He took a deep breath, wrestling with the emotions that surged within him, and began typing a response, careful to balance honesty with caution.

"I've missed you, Meera. It hasn't been the same without you."

What began as a hesitant exchange soon blossomed into a series of heartfelt conversations. They shared updates about their lives—Rahul's new job prospects and Meera's journey of recovery from her family's disapproval. As they reminisced about their favorite moments together, laughter filled the gaps that had formed during their separation. It felt as if the distance was slowly dissolving, allowing them to bridge the gap that had once seemed insurmountable.

As the days turned into weeks, their conversations grew deeper, exploring not just their lives but their feelings for one another. Rahul felt a renewed sense of connection, as if the flame of their love was being gently fanned back to life. He often found himself smiling at his phone, lost in thoughts of what could be, while Meera expressed her own longing for their relationship to heal.

One evening, after sharing a particularly nostalgic message about a college festival they had attended together, a wave of courage surged within Rahul. He made a bold decision, typing with a mix of excitement and trepidation. "How about we meet?" he sent, his heart pounding as he hit the send button. The moment felt monumental, and he held his breath, waiting for her response.

Moments later, Meera replied, her excitement palpable. "Yes! I'd love that! Where should we meet?"

They decided on a quaint café in the city, a place that held cherished memories of their carefree college days. As the day approached, Rahul felt a whirlwind of nerves and exhilaration. The thought of seeing Meera again after everything was both thrilling and terrifying. The night before their meeting, he replayed memories in his mind, wondering how their reunion would unfold. Would the spark still be there? Would they be able to navigate the complexities of their relationship after everything that had happened?

When the day finally arrived, Rahul arrived at the café early, anticipation buzzing in the air. The familiar scent of freshly brewed coffee and baked goods wafted through the air, mingling with the chatter of other patrons. As he sat at a table near the window, he felt a whirlwind of emotions—the joy of seeing her, the fear of reopening old wounds, and the hope that their connection could be rekindled.

Minutes felt like hours as he waited, his mind racing with possibilities. And then, he saw her. Meera walked in, looking radiant, her smile lighting up the room. Time seemed to stand still as their eyes locked. In that moment, all the months of separation melted away, and it felt as if they had never been apart.

"Rahul!" she exclaimed, rushing to his side. They embraced, and the warmth of her presence enveloped him like a familiar blanket. He breathed in the comforting scent of her hair, the scent he had missed so dearly.

"Meera," he whispered, pulling back to look into her eyes. The depth of emotion in her gaze spoke volumes about the love that still lingered between them. There were unspoken words, unshed tears, and countless memories behind those eyes.

They spent the afternoon reminiscing about their shared experiences—laughing about inside jokes, recalling moments of silliness, and sharing updates about their lives. The café buzzed around them, but it felt as though they were in their own world, untouched by the chaos beyond the walls. Each story, each shared memory, served as a reminder of the bond they had built over the years, a bond that had weathered storms and survived the harshest of separations.

As the sun began to set, casting a warm glow over the café, they found themselves lost in conversation, discussing their hopes and dreams for the future. The shadows of the past still lingered, but they spoke about the possibilities ahead, breathing life into dreams they had once shared.

"Can we make this work?" Meera asked, her voice soft yet filled with determination. "I don't want to lose you again."

Rahul nodded, feeling the weight of her words resonate within him. "I want that too. We can take it one step at a time."

With that promise, the flame of their love flickered to life once more. They had both endured so much, but now they stood together, ready to face whatever challenges lay ahead. This reunion marked the beginning of a new chapter—one filled with hope, healing, and the promise of rekindled love.

As they left the café hand in hand, a sense of peace enveloped them. The past might have been tumultuous, but in that moment, they knew they were stronger together. The warmth of their connection wrapped around them like a protective cocoon, shielding them from the uncertainties that awaited.

"Let's not rush into things," Rahul suggested, his voice steady yet gentle. "We should take our time to rebuild what we lost."

Meera smiled, her eyes sparkling with understanding. "I agree. We can start by being there for each other, just like before."

In the following weeks, they spent time reconnecting, not just through messages but also in person. They explored the city together, visited their old haunts, and slowly began to weave the threads of their relationship back together. Every meeting was filled with laughter, shared glances, and the growing realization that they had not only found each other again but also discovered themselves in the process.

Yet, the shadows of their past were never too far behind. They had to navigate the complexities of their relationship—Meera's family's disapproval still loomed over them like a dark cloud. Rahul often found himself caught in moments of doubt, wondering if they could truly overcome the obstacles that had once driven them apart.

One evening, as they strolled through a park, Rahul voiced his fears. "What if things don't change with your family? What if they never accept us?"

Meera stopped, turning to face him. "I won't let fear dictate our future. I'll talk to them. I'll show them how much we mean to each other."

Rahul admired her determination, yet he couldn't shake off the worry that clung to him. They sat on a bench, watching the sunset paint the sky in hues of orange and pink. "I believe in us, Meera," he said, his voice low. "But I also don't want you to face this alone."

"We're in this together," she replied, her hand squeezing his. "No matter what happens, we'll find a way."

And with that promise, they sealed their commitment to one another—a pact born from love and strengthened by the trials they had endured. They were no longer just two individuals navigating the storm; they were partners, willing to fight for their love against all odds.

As time passed, they discovered new layers of their relationship, growing together and allowing their love to flourish in ways they had never imagined. Their bond deepened as they shared their dreams, fears, and aspirations. They learned to communicate openly, expressing not just their love but also their vulnerabilities, fears, and hopes.

One morning, as they sat together in a café, sipping coffee and planning their day, Rahul couldn't help but smile. "I never thought we would be here again, sharing moments like this."

Meera smiled back, her eyes shining with warmth. "Life has a way of bringing us back to where we belong."

In that moment, Rahul realized that they had indeed found their way back to each other. The journey was far from over, but they were ready to face whatever challenges lay ahead, armed with love, resilience, and the unwavering belief that they could overcome anything together.

As they left the café hand in hand, the sun shone brightly overhead, illuminating the path before them. They walked into their future, ready.

ᗑᗑᗑ

"Resilience and self-improvement turn setbacks into steps toward growth, as our habits, mindset, and quest for knowledge reveal our true potential for a fulfilling life."

SIX

THE BIG MOVE

"In every ending, there's a new beginning. It's at the end of the journey that we discover the depth of the adventure. "
- Morgan Freeman

After their heartfelt reunion, Rahul and Meera felt a renewed sense of purpose. They began to navigate their relationship with a fresh perspective, filled with hope and determination. Their daily conversations grew into plans for the future, and soon they were discussing the possibility of a new beginning—together.

One evening, during a video call illuminated by the soft glow of their screens, Meera's voice danced through the air, infused with excitement. "Why don't we move to a bigger city?" she suggested, her eyes sparkling with enthusiasm. "Somewhere we can both find opportunities and start fresh. I've always wanted to explore new horizons."

Rahul paused, contemplating the idea. A part of him hesitated, still haunted by the shadows of the past, but another part felt invigorated by the prospect of building a life with Meera. "You mean like Mumbai?" he replied, a mix of excitement and anxiety flooding his thoughts.

"Exactly! It's a vibrant city with so much to offer. We could both find jobs and maybe even share an apartment," she said, her enthusiasm palpable as she envisioned their future.

As they continued to discuss the possibility, the idea began to feel like a beacon of hope. It would be a chance to create new memories, away from the judgments and misunderstandings that had clouded their past. "We can carve out a life that's uniquely ours," Meera added, her voice full of determination.

"Let's do it," Rahul finally said, a grin breaking across his face. "Let's start this adventure together."

With their decision made, they dove headfirst into planning their move. Over the next few weeks, they meticulously researched neighborhoods, job prospects, and the logistics of relocating. Every evening was filled with animated discussions, laughter, and the kind of hopeful dreaming that comes with the promise of new beginnings.

"Do you think we'll find a nice apartment?" Meera asked one night, her voice tinged with excitement.

"I'm sure we will! We'll make it our own little sanctuary," Rahul replied, imagining the cozy space they would create together.

Their conversations often flowed into late-night brainstorming sessions, and they even created a shared digital folder filled with apartment listings, dream destinations, and things they wanted to explore in the city. As the days turned into weeks, the anticipation grew, filling their hearts with the thrill of the unknown.

Once they arrived in Mumbai, the city engulfed them with its energy and chaos. The streets buzzed with life—people bustling about, street vendors calling out, and the distant sound of waves crashing against the shore. It was a stark contrast to their previous lives, and yet it felt exhilarating, like stepping onto a stage where anything was possible.

"Welcome to the city of dreams!" Meera exclaimed as they stepped out of the cab, taking in the vibrant atmosphere. The sunlight bathed everything in a warm glow, and Rahul felt the weight of possibility settling on his shoulders.

They settled into a cozy apartment in a lively neighborhood filled with cafes, parks, and the laughter of children playing nearby. The walls became their canvas, echoing with laughter and the small kitchen filled with the aroma of shared meals. Rahul often found himself smiling as he watched Meera move about the apartment, her spirit vibrant and infectious.

In those early days, they found joy in the mundane—the sound of the kettle boiling, the smell of fresh paint as they decorated their new home, and the warmth of each other's presence in the small spaces they created.

"Home is not just a place; it's a feeling," Meera said one evening as they snuggled on the couch, surrounded by boxes yet to be unpacked. "And I feel at home with you."

As they settled in, both began job hunting. Rahul pursued opportunities in his field, while Meera explored her passion for design. The initial excitement of their new life fueled their motivation, and they embraced the challenges of the bustling city together.

"Have you seen this job listing?" Meera said one afternoon, showing Rahul her laptop screen. "It's perfect for you!"

Rahul smiled, feeling the warmth of her encouragement. "And look at this one! It's for a design firm that aligns with your goals."

However, as time passed, the reality of their circumstances began to weigh heavily on them. The pressure to find stable jobs was daunting, and there were days when the search felt endless. Doubts crept in like unwelcome guests, and the thrill of their new life began to wane under the stress of uncertainty.

One evening, after a particularly long day of interviews and rejections, they returned home, exhausted but determined. They collapsed onto the balcony, overlooking the twinkling city lights. Meera turned to Rahul, her expression resolute. "I know things are tough right now, but I believe in us. We've made it this far together."

Her words resonated deeply, like a soothing balm to his frayed nerves. "You're right. We've come through so much. We can't let this city or anything else tear us apart." He reached for her hand, feeling a surge of love and gratitude.

"Together, we are unstoppable," she replied, squeezing his hand tightly.

As they faced these challenges, their bond grew stronger, a testament to their commitment to one another. With every setback, they found solace in each other's presence, reminding themselves that they were not alone in this journey.

"We'll get through this," Rahul reassured her one night as they sat on their balcony, the night air filled with the sounds of the city. "Our love is worth fighting for."

Then, one day, fortune smiled upon them. Meera received a call for a design position at a local firm. Her excitement was palpable as she shared the news with Rahul, her voice trembling with disbelief. "I got the job! I can't believe it!"

Rahul felt a rush of pride swell within him. "That's amazing, Meera! I knew you could do it!" They celebrated that evening, their hearts filled with hope for the future, laughter spilling into the night air like a sweet melody.

In the weeks that followed, Rahul also found a promising job opportunity. It wasn't just a job; it was a chance to step into a role that aligned with his career aspirations. The couple felt a sense of relief wash over them as they settled into their new routines, both working toward their dreams side by side.

As the months passed, their love flourished in the vibrant city. They explored the streets of Mumbai together, discovering hidden gems and enjoying the rich cultural tapestry around them. They attended local festivals, danced in the rain, and shared countless moments that deepened their connection.

"Look at the colors of this festival!" Meera exclaimed one day as they walked through the streets adorned with vibrant decorations. "It feels like we're living in a painting!"

"It's beautiful," Rahul agreed, pulling her closer as they navigated through the throngs of people. "Just like you."

However, just as they began to feel secure in their new life, whispers from the past began to surface. Meera's parents, having learned of their move, reached out through social media, leaving messages filled with anger and resentment. They threatened to come to Mumbai, insisting they would not allow their daughter to be with someone they deemed unworthy.

As Meera read the messages, her heart sank. She turned to Rahul, fear etched across her face. "What if they come here? I don't want them to ruin everything we've built."

Rahul took a deep breath, wrapping his arms around her, feeling her tremble. "We'll face it together. We've overcome so much already. We can't let their anger dictate our lives."

Together, they devised a plan. They would remain steadfast in their commitment to each other, regardless of the challenges that lay ahead. Their love had survived the storm of misunderstandings and betrayal, and now it would withstand the pressure of external threats.

"It's time we take a stand," Meera said, her voice steady. "I won't let them control my life anymore."

"Exactly," Rahul affirmed, his resolve strengthening. "We're not kids anymore. We can make our own choices."

That night, as they lay in bed, Rahul pulled Meera close, feeling the rhythm of her heartbeat against his chest. "Remember what we talked about? Love isn't just about the easy times. It's about weathering the storms together."

Meera smiled, feeling reassured in his embrace. "I'm glad we're in this together. No matter what happens, we'll find a way."

This chapter encapsulates the joy of new beginnings, the trials of adulthood, and the unwavering bond that Rahul and Meera share. As they build their life in Mumbai, they find strength in each other, prepared to face whatever challenges come their way.

"Life is not measured by the number of breaths we take, but by the moments that take our breath away," Rahul whispered one evening as they watched the city skyline from their balcony, the horizon kissed by the setting sun.

Meera smiled, resting her head on his shoulder. "And every moment with you is a treasure I hold close to my heart."

In that moment, surrounded by the vibrant chaos of Mumbai, they realized that their love was not just a refuge; it was a force that propelled them forward, inspiring them to dream bigger and fight harder for the life they envisioned together. As they prepared to face whatever lay ahead, their hearts were intertwined, a testament to the power of love and resilience.

ᐁᐁᐁ

"Reconnecting and resolving misunderstandings can reignite motivation for personal growth, proving that sometimes, a second chance can fuel our journey towards becoming our best selves."

SEVEN

SHATTERED DREAMS

As Rahul and Meera settled into their lives in Mumbai, the initial excitement of their new beginning began to unravel like the frayed ends of a tapestry. The vibrant streets that had once inspired them now felt burdened by the weight of external expectations. In the soft glow of their apartment, they tried to create a cocoon of warmth and love, but reality crept in with its harsh demands.

The couple often found solace in their shared routines. Each morning, they would sip tea together, surrounded by the gentle hum of the city waking up. "It's just us against the world," Rahul would say, wrapping his arm around Meera as they watched the sun rise over the horizon. As Rahul and Meera settled into their lives in Mumbai, the initial excitement of their new beginning began to unravel like the frayed ends of a tapestry. The vibrant streets that had once inspired them now felt burdened by the weight of external expectations. In the soft glow of their apartment, they tried to create a cocoon of warmth and love, but reality crept in with its harsh demands.

The couple often found solace in their shared routines. Each morning, they would sip tea together, surrounded by the gentle hum of the city waking up. "It's just us against the world," Rahul would say, wrapping his arm around Meera as they watched the sun rise over the horizon. They believed in the dreams they had painted together, a canvas filled with aspirations that stretched far beyond the concrete jungle that surrounded them.

Yet, unbeknownst to them, Meera's parents were soon to discover her whereabouts. The revelation sent shockwaves through their family, igniting a fire of anger and concern that would soon consume the couple. Meera's father, a police officer with deeply rooted beliefs about honor and reputation, was furious when he learned that his daughter was living with Rahul. To him, this was not merely a personal decision; it was a public affront to their family's name and values.

Meera's life in Mumbai was a juxtaposition of dreams and struggles. Every day, she faced the city's relentless pace, where dreams often collided with harsh realities. The vibrant streets that had once filled her with excitement now felt like a labyrinth of expectations. As she ventured into the corporate world, she found herself navigating a minefield of competition and ambition.

"Success is not just about talent; it's about resilience," she often reminded herself as she trudged through crowded train stations, packed with commuters. The daily grind was a test of endurance, yet she pushed through, inspired by the dream of building a future with Rahul.

But the emotional weight of her parents' disapproval loomed large. The moment Meera received a call from her father, she felt a cold shiver run down her spine. "You have brought shame upon us," he thundered through the phone, his voice a mix of fury and disappointment. "You need to choose your family over this boy." Meera felt the weight of his words heavy on her chest, suffocating her spirit. In Mumbai, she learned that sometimes love is overshadowed by familial duty.

Her heart ached as she grappled with her loyalty to her parents versus her love for Rahul. "I'm happy, Dad! I love him!" she protested, her voice trembling with desperation. But her father's anger echoed in her ears like a relentless drumbeat.

Days turned into restless nights as Meera found herself caught in an emotional whirlwind. The initial joy of being with Rahul faded as the reality of her parents' disapproval settled in. Each time her phone chimed with another message from her father, a sense of dread washed over her. In this bustling metropolis, the noise was overwhelming, drowning out the whispers of their love.

Mumbai, often referred to as the city of dreams, is a character in itself—a city that never sleeps, pulsating with life and ambition. Yet, beneath its vibrant surface lies a struggle shared by many. Rahul, too, found himself grappling with his aspirations. He worked long hours at a startup, pouring his heart and soul into every project, yet facing the harsh reality of job insecurity and constant competition.

"Dreams don't work unless you do," he often reminded himself as he navigated the challenges of the corporate world. Each day was a battle against the odds, yet his determination never wavered. He wanted to build a future not only for himself but for Meera, a life filled with laughter, love, and mutual support.

As weeks passed, the couple often walked through the bustling streets of Mumbai, hand in hand, searching for solace amid the chaos. They found little pockets of joy—a street vendor selling fresh vada pav, the aroma of spices wafting through the air, and the laughter of children playing in the nearby park. Yet, even in these moments, the shadow of Meera's family loomed large.

One evening, after a particularly heated phone call, Meera broke down in tears. Rahul sat beside her, trying to offer comfort, but the tension in the room was palpable. "I can't keep living like this," she confessed, her voice shaking. "I don't want to lose you, but my parents are relentless."

"Meera, remember," Rahul said gently, "the struggles we face today will only make our love stronger tomorrow. Every challenge is an opportunity for growth." His words, meant to inspire, felt inadequate in the face of her familial obligations.

As the weeks turned into months, the conflict intensified. Meera received calls and messages from her parents, each one more threatening than the last. They expressed their disappointment and painted a grim picture of the consequences of defiance. The emotional toll began to weigh heavily on her, causing her to withdraw from Rahul.

The couple's apartment, once filled with laughter and dreams, now felt like a cage. They sat in silence, the air thick with unspoken words and unresolved feelings. Rahul felt the weight of her struggles, yet he could do little but offer his unwavering support.

"Maybe we should take a break," he suggested one night, his voice tentative, hoping to ease the pressure on her. "I don't want you to lose your family over me."

"No, Rahul. I don't want to lose you either. But I can't see a way out of this," Meera responded, tears brimming in her eyes.

Then came the fateful night that would change everything. Meera's father, determined to assert control, decided to confront Rahul directly. Enlisting the help of a few officers, his colleagues, he believed they could intimidate the boy who dared to love his daughter.

As Rahul left the library late one evening, lost in thought about his future with Meera, he was ambushed. The city was quiet, the streets empty, illuminated only by the flickering streetlights. Suddenly, he found himself cornered in an alley.

"Rahul!" he heard a voice call out. He turned to see Meera's father and two officers standing before him, their faces twisted in anger. "You think you can take my daughter away from me?" her father shouted, rage boiling over. "You will regret this!"

Before Rahul could respond, the officers moved in, shoving him against the wall. Panic surged through him, a primal fear coursing through his veins. "This isn't necessary!" he pleaded, his voice shaking. But they were not interested in dialogue. The confrontation escalated quickly; punches were thrown, and Rahul found himself on the ground, surrounded by hostility.

The physical pain was sharp, but the emotional agony cut deeper. As he lay there, bruised and bewildered, he couldn't shake the feeling of betrayal. The man he had once trusted as a father figure now stood before him as an enemy. It was a moment that would haunt him, a reminder of how love can quickly turn into despair when faced with external forces.

After the attack, Rahul struggled to find solace. He felt defeated, both physically and emotionally. The person he had loved most was now tied to a family that viewed him as an intruder. The dreams they had built together felt shattered, like glass scattered across the floor. He questioned everything: Was their love strong enough to withstand the pressure? Or had he misjudged the depth of her commitment?

Meera, upon hearing about the incident, was devastated. She rushed to Rahul's side, her heart aching at the sight of him wounded and broken. "I'm so sorry, Rahul. I never wanted this," she cried, tears streaming down her cheeks.

In that moment, their shared pain became a mirror reflecting the reality of their situation. "I don't know how we can fight this," Meera whispered, her voice trembling. "I feel trapped."

"Meera, I love you," Rahul said, his voice hoarse. "But we can't let this tear us apart. We have to find a way to navigate this."

Despite her sorrow, Meera felt trapped. Her loyalty to her family was strong, and she feared their anger would only escalate. She found herself standing at a crossroads: continue to fight for the love that had brought her so much happiness or succumb to the pressures of her family, risking everything she had built with Rahul.

That night, as they sat together in silence, Rahul's heart raced with conflicting emotions. The warmth that had once enveloped their love was now chilled by the fear of loss. "Maybe a break is what we need to clear our heads," he suggested hesitantly. "I don't want you to lose your family over me."

Meera's eyes widened, and she shook her head vehemently. "No, Rahul. I don't want to lose you either. But I can't see a way out of this." The pain in her eyes mirrored his own, a reflection of the love that had been overshadowed by fear.

In the days that followed, the couple struggled to find their footing. The dreams they had shared began to feel like distant echoes, drowned out by the noise of external conflicts. Meera felt torn apart, caught between her love for Rahul and her desire to maintain her family's approval. They often walked through the bustling streets of Mumbai in silence, each lost in their thoughts, their hands brushing against each other like fleeting shadows.

One afternoon, they found themselves sitting in a park, watching families play, couples laugh, and friends share moments of joy. "Look at that couple," Meera

However, unbeknownst to them, Meera's parents were soon to discover her whereabouts. The revelation sent shockwaves through their family, igniting a fire of anger and concern that would soon consume the couple. Meera's father, a police officer with deeply rooted beliefs about honor and reputation, was furious when he learned that his daughter was living with Rahul. To him, this was not merely a personal decision; it was a public affront to their family's name and values.

The moment Meera received a call from her father, she felt a cold shiver run down her spine. "You have brought shame upon us," he thundered through the phone, his voice a mix of fury and disappointment. "You need to choose your family over this boy." Meera felt the weight of his words heavy on her chest, suffocating her spirit.

Her heart ached as she grappled with her loyalty to her parents versus her love for Rahul. "I'm happy, Dad! I love him!" she protested, her voice trembling with desperation. But her father's anger echoed in her ears like a relentless drumbeat.

Days turned into restless nights as Meera found herself caught in an emotional whirlwind. The initial joy of being with Rahul faded as the reality of her parents' disapproval settled in. Each time her phone chimed with another message from her father, a sense of dread washed over her.

One evening, after a particularly heated phone call, Meera broke down in tears. Rahul sat beside her, trying to offer comfort, but the tension in the room was palpable. "I can't keep living like this," she confessed, her voice shaking. "I don't want to lose you, but my parents are relentless."

Rahul felt a deep sense of helplessness wash over him. "We can fight this together," he pleaded, holding her hands in his. "We've come so far, Meera. Don't let them dictate our lives."

"But what if they come for you? What if they hurt you?" Meera's eyes shimmered with unshed tears, and Rahul could see the cracks forming in their once unshakeable bond. The pressure from her family was suffocating her, and he feared for their future.

As days turned into weeks, the conflict intensified. Meera received calls and messages from her parents, each one more threatening than the last. They expressed their disappointment and painted a grim picture of the consequences of defiance. The emotional toll began to weigh heavily on her, causing her to withdraw from Rahul.

They would sit in silence, the air thick with unspoken words and unresolved feelings. What had once been an apartment filled with laughter and light now felt like a cage. The joyous moments they once shared began to fade, replaced by the looming presence of her family's disapproval.

"Maybe we should take a break," Rahul suggested one night, his voice tentative, hoping to ease the pressure on her. "I don't want you to lose your family over me."

Meera shook her head vehemently. "No, Rahul. I don't want to lose you either. But I can't see a way out of this."

Then came the fateful night that would change everything. Meera's father, determined to assert control, decided to confront Rahul directly. Enlisting the help of a few officers, his colleagues, he believed they could intimidate the boy who dared to love his daughter.

As Rahul left the library late one evening, lost in thought about his future with Meera, he was ambushed. The city was quiet, the streets empty, illuminated only by the flickering streetlights. Suddenly, he found himself cornered in an alley.

"Rahul!" he heard a voice call out. He turned to see Meera's father and two officers standing before him, their faces twisted in anger. "You think you can take my daughter away from me?" her father shouted, rage boiling over. "You will regret this!"

Before Rahul could respond, the officers moved in, shoving him against the wall. Panic surged through him, a primal fear that coursed through his veins. "This isn't necessary!" he pleaded, his voice shaking. But they were not interested in dialogue. The confrontation escalated quickly; punches were thrown, and Rahul found himself on the ground, surrounded by hostility.

The physical pain was sharp, but the emotional agony cut deeper. As he lay there, bruised and bewildered, he couldn't shake the feeling of betrayal. The man he had once trusted as a father figure now stood before him as an enemy. It was a moment that would haunt him, a reminder of how love can quickly turn into despair when faced with external forces.

After the attack, Rahul struggled to find solace. He felt defeated, both physically and emotionally. The person he had loved most was now tied to a family that viewed him as an intruder. The dreams they had built together felt shattered, like glass scattered across the floor. He questioned everything: Was their love strong enough to withstand the pressure? Or had he misjudged the depth of her commitment?

Meera, upon hearing about the incident, was devastated. She rushed to Rahul's side, her heart aching at the sight of him wounded and broken. "I'm so sorry, Rahul. I never wanted this," she cried, tears streaming down her cheeks.

In that moment, their shared pain became a mirror reflecting the reality of their situation. "I don't know how we can fight this," Meera whispered, her voice trembling. "I feel trapped."

"Meera, I love you," Rahul said, his voice hoarse. "But we can't let this tear us apart. We have to find a way to navigate this."

Despite her sorrow, Meera felt trapped. Her loyalty to her family was strong, and she feared their anger would only escalate. She found herself standing at a crossroads: continue to fight for the love that had brought her so much happiness, or succumb to the pressures of her family, risking everything she had built with Rahul.

That night, as they sat together in silence, Rahul's heart raced with conflicting emotions. The warmth that had once enveloped their love was now chilled by the fear of loss. "Maybe a break is what we need to clear our heads," he suggested hesitantly. "I don't want you to lose your family over me."

Meera's eyes widened, and she shook her head vehemently. "No, Rahul. I don't want to lose you either. But I can't see a way out of this." The pain in her eyes mirrored his own, a reflection of the love that had been overshadowed by fear.

In the days that followed, the couple struggled to find their footing. The dreams they had shared began to feel like distant echoes, drowned out by the noise of external conflicts. Meera felt torn apart, caught between her love for Rahul and her desire to maintain her family's approval. They often walked through the bustling streets of Mumbai in silence, each lost in their thoughts, their hands brushing against each other like fleeting shadows.

"Look at that couple," Meera said one day, nodding toward a pair sitting on a park bench, sharing ice cream and laughter. "They look so happy."

"Yeah," Rahul replied, his heart aching. "But happiness feels like a distant memory for us right now."

The chapter closed on a bittersweet note, encapsulating the reality of their situation: love, once a source of joy, had transformed into a battlefield. The vibrant colors of their love story had faded to gray, leaving behind only the outlines of what once was. They were left grappling with shattered dreams, caught in a struggle that threatened to pull them apart forever.

As Meera lay awake one night, staring at the ceiling, she whispered to herself, "What do I really want?" The uncertainty loomed large in her mind, threatening to engulf her. And as she closed her eyes, she hoped for a glimmer of clarity in the darkness.

"Sometimes," Rahul mused, gazing out at the city skyline, "love isn't enough to conquer everything. But it's what we do with that love that defines us."

As they faced the darkness together, both Rahul and Meera knew that their love was being tested like never before, and the path ahead was fraught with uncertainty. Would they find the strength to overcome the shadows that threatened to consume them, or would the external forces tear them apart forever? The answer lay hidden in the heart of their love, waiting to be uncovered.

ᗡᗡᗡ

"Having a mentor is invaluable; they provide guidance, wisdom, and insight that can help navigate through challenges, accelerate personal and professional growth, and unlock potential we may not even realize we have."

EIGHT

LOST AND ALONE

In the aftermath of their heartbreaking separation, Rahul found himself adrift in a sea of despair. The vibrant city of Mumbai, once filled with promise and excitement, now felt suffocating and isolating. Every street he walked seemed to echo the laughter and love he had shared with Meera, amplifying his sense of loss. The towering skyscrapers that had once inspired him now loomed like specters, reminders of a life he could no longer grasp.

Each morning began with the same dull routine. Rahul would rise from his bed, the sheets still warm with the remnants of dreams that danced just beyond his reach. He would stare into the mirror, searching for the spark in his eyes that had been extinguished. He often muttered to himself, "The wound is where the light enters you," as if reminding himself that pain was an integral part of healing. Yet, each day felt like a battle against the darkness that had settled over his heart.

He buried himself in work, attempting to distract himself from the emotional pain that had become a constant companion. The office, once a place of collaboration and laughter, had transformed into a hollow space, echoing his solitude. Late nights became his refuge, where the dim glow of his computer screen illuminated his fatigue. Yet, no matter how hard he tried to drown out the memories, they lingered like shadows, refusing to fade. The sound of laughter from the nearby café would seep through the walls, a cruel reminder of the joy he once knew.

Weeks turned into months, and his friends grew increasingly concerned about his withdrawn behavior. He missed gatherings, avoided phone calls, and declined invitations with vague excuses. The vibrant social life he once enjoyed became a distant memory as he isolated himself in his apartment, preferring solitude over the company of others. The walls that had once embraced their laughter now felt like a prison, closing in on him with every tick of the clock.

On particularly lonely nights, Rahul would sit on his balcony, gazing at the stars as tears streamed down his face. He would whisper into the silence, "Why did it have to end this way?" wishing for answers that never came. Each tear felt like a tribute to the love he had lost, a river of grief flowing into the vast ocean of his despair. The emotional turmoil left him feeling hollow, as if a piece of his soul had been ripped away.

One evening, as the sun dipped below the horizon, painting the sky in hues of orange and purple, he sat on a park bench, lost in thought. A couple nearby laughed, their joy a stark contrast to his solitude. The woman leaned her head on her partner's shoulder, and the simple act of tenderness twisted the knife in his heart. He closed his eyes, wishing he could turn back time, to relive those moments of love and laughter with Meera.

Weeks passed, and the emotional weight grew heavier. Overwhelmed by feelings of loneliness, Rahul made a spontaneous decision to book a flight to London. He had always dreamed of visiting the city, but now it felt like an escape—an opportunity to distance himself from the memories that suffocated him. As he boarded the plane, he felt a flicker of hope. Perhaps a change of scenery would bring clarity, a chance to breathe without the heavy chains of grief.

In London, he wandered through the bustling streets, each corner revealing a new sight, yet his heart remained anchored in the past. One rainy afternoon, as he stood beneath an awning, watching droplets dance on the pavement, he recalled the day he and Meera had strolled through a similar rain in Mumbai, their laughter blending with the sound of raindrops.

"In the midst of winter, I found there was, within me, an invincible summer," he whispered to himself, recalling a quote by Albert Camus, but feeling more like winter than summer. The memories of Meera flooded back—her infectious laughter, the way her eyes sparkled with joy, and the warmth of her presence.

In that moment of solitude, Rahul felt an overwhelming urge to express his emotions. He pulled out a small notebook and began to write:

"In the quiet of the night, when stars softly weep,
I walk these lonely streets, where memories seep.
In every shadow, I see your face,
In every whisper of the wind, I feel your grace."

Each word flowed from his heart, a cathartic release of the pain he had carried for so long. As he continued to write, he found solace in poetry, a way to channel his grief into something beautiful.

Rahul often returned to their favorite spots in the city, where echoes of their laughter still resonated. The quaint little café where they shared their dreams over steaming cups of chai, the park where they had carved their initials into the bark of an ancient tree, and the bookstore where they had spent countless hours lost in words. Each place was a bittersweet reminder of the love that had felt so real yet had been so easily shattered.

One evening, he found himself in that café, staring out at the busy street. The aroma of fresh coffee filled the air, mingling with the memories that enveloped him. He could almost hear Meera's laughter, feel the warmth of her hand in his. He closed his eyes, allowing the memories to wash over him.

"The greatest sin is to think yourself weak," Swami Vivekananda's words echoed in his mind, igniting a spark of determination within him. He realized that feeling lost didn't mean he had to remain in despair.

In a moment of vulnerability, he confided in a close friend, Priya, during a rare lunch break. "I don't know how to move on. I feel like I've lost a part of myself," he admitted, his voice barely above a whisper. Priya listened intently, her heart aching for him. "You loved deeply, Rahul. It's okay to grieve that love. But you need to find a way to heal and rediscover yourself."

Though her words resonated, they felt distant. Healing seemed an insurmountable task, a mountain too steep to climb. Rahul appreciated her concern but felt stuck in a cycle of despair. He wanted to move on, but every attempt felt futile, as if he were running in place. His heart carried the weight of memories that felt like lead, anchoring him in the past.

On lonely evenings, he found himself scrolling through social media, inevitably stumbling upon photos of Meera. Each image was a dagger to his heart, reigniting the pain he thought he had buried. He saw her smiling with friends, attending events, and living a life that seemed untouched by the grief that enveloped him. The contrast was stark and painful, as he felt like a ghost in a world he no longer belonged to.

"Arise, awake, and stop not till the goal is reached," he reminded himself, channeling the spirit of Swami Vivekananda. It was a call to action, a reminder that he could forge his own path forward.

As days turned into weeks, Rahul found himself caught in a delicate dance between pain and healing. He began to find small pieces of himself again through photography, the art allowing him to express the emotions he struggled to voice. Yet the pain of lost love lingered in the background, a constant reminder of what he had once held dear.

During a particularly poignant moment, as he stood in front of the iconic Tower Bridge, he felt a rush of inspiration. He took a deep breath and wrote another poem:

"In this city of dreams, I wander alone,
Searching for solace, a place to call home.
But through the fog of despair, your light shines bright,
Guiding me gently, like stars in the night."

These moments of reflection and creativity were slowly stitching the wounds in his heart, reminding him that even in loneliness, there was beauty to be found.

Through inspiring stories of others like Anil, he learned that loneliness could be transformed into an opportunity for growth and connection. Rahul recognized the importance of reaching out, seeking help, and finding joy in the little things—whether through helping others, engaging in new activities, or simply appreciating the beauty around him.

As he pondered his journey, Rahul understood that every experience, whether joyful or painful, contributed to his growth. The scars he carried were not marks of defeat but symbols of resilience. They were reminders of love, laughter, and life lessons learned along the way.

He stood in front of the River Thames, feeling the gentle breeze against his skin. In that moment, he made a promise to himself: he would no longer allow loneliness to define him. "The strongest man is he who is able to conquer himself," Swami Vivekananda's words resonated within him, filling him with resolve.

Embracing Vulnerability: Being open to pain is an essential part of healing. It's through acknowledging our struggles that we can find strength and resilience.

Finding Purpose: In times of despair, connecting with others and giving back can reignite our sense of purpose. Helping others often leads to healing within ourselves.

Redefining Relationships: Love is not always about possession. Sometimes, letting go and wishing for the happiness of the ones we love is the most selfless act.

The Journey of Self-Discovery: Life is a series of transformations, and every end can lead to a new beginning.

With newfound determination, Rahul walked away from the river, ready to embrace whatever came next. The city felt different now—full of possibilities rather than reminders of his past. He was learning to carry Meera's memory with him not as a weight but as a source of inspiration, propelling him toward his future.

ᕭᕭᕭ

"Embracing our imperfections and viewing challenges as opportunities for growth leads to true self-discovery and fulfillment, teaching us that courage, not the absence of fear, defines our path to realizing our potential."

NINE
A NEW BEGINNING IN LONDON

"Success is not final, failure is not fatal: It is the courage to continue that counts. "
- Winston Churchill

Seeking solace from the overwhelming grief that had consumed him since his separation from Meera, Rahul made a bold decision to move to London. The vibrant city, known for its diversity and bustling energy, offered him the hope of a fresh start—a chance to escape the memories that haunted him in Mumbai. With a heavy heart but a determination to rebuild his life, he packed his bags and boarded a plane, leaving behind the shadows of his past.

As the plane ascended, he gazed out the window at the shrinking landscape below, a patchwork of memories woven into the very fabric of that land. The tears he had shed for Meera were a poignant reminder of the love he had lost. Yet, beneath the pain, there was a flicker of hope—a whisper that told him change could lead to renewal.

Upon arriving in London, Rahul was captivated by the city's charm. The historic architecture, lively streets, and eclectic culture provided a stark contrast to the isolation he had felt for months. Every corner he turned revealed something new, an adventure waiting to unfold. The double-decker buses, the sound of laughter wafting from nearby pubs, and the vibrant street markets filled his senses, drawing him into a world of possibilities.

In those early days, Rahul found solace in exploring London's rich tapestry of life. He spent his days wandering through parks, visiting art galleries, and immersing himself in the local culture. One particularly crisp autumn afternoon, he visited the iconic Borough Market. The rich aroma of spices and fresh produce enveloped him, and he watched as vendors enthusiastically shared their culinary stories. Sampling street food, he felt a warmth in his chest—a reminder that life, despite its challenges, was still full of beauty.

"Every dish tells a story," he thought as he relished the flavors of a spicy chaat, reminiscent of the bustling street food scenes in Mumbai. Yet, even amidst these vibrant experiences, the echoes of his past often crept in, reminding him of Meera.

In the heart of London, he found comfort in photography, using his camera to capture the essence of the city. He wandered through the lush greenery of Hyde Park, where the vibrant colors of the autumn leaves danced in the breeze. Children played with abandon, their laughter ringing through the air, and street performers showcased their talents, filling the atmosphere with a sense of joy. Each click of the shutter was an attempt to freeze moments in time, a way to document his new journey while keeping a piece of his old life alive.

Yet, the vibrant experiences of London often stirred memories of India—a land filled with familial love, childhood friendships, and the intoxicating vibrancy of Mumbai. Rahul reminisced about the bustling local trains, the aroma of masala chai wafting through the air, and the warm, inviting streets filled with familiar faces. He thought of Meera's laughter ringing out like a sweet melody, echoing through the busy markets, and the late-night conversations under starlit skies.

One evening, as he strolled along the Thames, the shimmering lights reflected on the water reminded him of the festive Diwali celebrations back home. He could almost hear the laughter of friends and family, the sounds of firecrackers bursting in the sky, illuminating the night. "Life in Mumbai was chaotic yet beautiful," he mused, a sense of nostalgia washing over him. The richness of his past felt like a tapestry, each thread intricately woven with memories.

Despite the enchantment of London, Rahul faced significant struggles. The high cost of living weighed heavily on his shoulders. Finding a job proved to be a daunting task, especially as he navigated the complexities of a foreign work environment. He spent countless hours scrolling through job listings, tailoring his resume, and preparing for interviews. The rejections piled up like autumn leaves, each one stinging more than the last.

His mornings began early, as he sought out opportunities, wandering into coffee shops to use their Wi-Fi and apply for jobs. With each passing day, the excitement of exploration gave way to the harsh reality of financial constraints. He often found himself daydreaming about his life in India, where familial support was more prevalent, and community ties were strong. Here, in this sprawling metropolis, he felt isolated, surrounded by the bustle of life yet disconnected from it.

One evening, after another fruitless day of job hunting, he sat on a park bench in Greenwich, watching the sunset paint the sky in hues of orange and purple. The beauty of the moment was bittersweet. "How did it come to this?" he whispered to himself, grappling with the weight of loneliness. "I came here for a fresh start, yet it feels like a never-ending struggle."

However, amid the challenges, Rahul found solace in the kindness of strangers. One day, while he was at a café, he struck up a conversation with a fellow patron named Tom. A friendly Englishman with a passion for travel, Tom shared stories of his adventures around the globe. Their discussions turned into a weekly tradition, and Rahul found comfort in their growing friendship. Tom introduced him to local culture, inviting him to concerts, art shows, and pub trivia nights. Through these experiences, Rahul began to see the beauty of human connection in a city filled with transient lives.

As he settled into his new routine, he began to appreciate the small joys of life in London. A trip to the Southbank Centre for an art exhibition one rainy afternoon ignited a spark within him. The vibrant colors of contemporary art reminded him of the rich heritage of Indian art, and he felt a sense of belonging. "Art transcends boundaries," he thought, "much like love."

On weekends, he joined free walking tours that unveiled hidden gems around the city—quaint bookshops, historic landmarks, and lush gardens. Each new discovery felt like a celebration of life, a testament to resilience and the beauty of the human spirit.

Yet, amidst the excitement of his new life, memories of Meera often intruded upon his thoughts. The laughter they had shared, the dreams they had woven together, and the love that once felt so alive lingered like ghosts, refusing to fade completely. On quiet nights, when the city was bathed in the soft glow of streetlights, he would find himself longing for her presence, questioning whether he would ever truly be able to move on.

One fateful day, while exploring a local market, Rahul felt a sense of déjà vu as he turned a corner and caught sight of a familiar face. There, amidst the bustling crowd, stood Meera. Time seemed to freeze as his heart raced. She looked radiant, her laughter ringing like a melody through the air, and she was surrounded by a group of friends. The sight of her, seemingly thriving and happy, struck him with a mix of emotions that he had not anticipated.

As he stood frozen in place, watching her, a wave of conflicting feelings washed over him. On one hand, he was overwhelmed by the joy of seeing her again; her laughter, her smile, everything that had once captivated him felt alive in that moment. On the other hand, a deep sadness settled in his chest. She was with someone else—a reality he had to confront. The image of her happiness, now shared with another man, felt like a sharp reminder of what he had lost.

Meera's husband stood beside her, a kind and gentle presence who seemed to genuinely care for her. Watching their interaction stirred a sense of protectiveness within Rahul; he wanted her to be happy, but the sight of her sharing moments with another man felt like a betrayal of their past. His heart ached as he remembered the plans they had made, the love they had shared, and the dreams they had envisioned together.

Summoning all his courage, Rahul took a few steps closer, hoping to catch her attention. As if sensing his presence, Meera turned and locked eyes with him. For a brief moment, time stood still. Recognition flickered across her face, followed by a mix of surprise and emotion. Rahul's heart raced, and he felt the familiar pull of love intertwining with the pain of their separation.

"Rahul?" Meera's voice was soft, almost incredulous, as if she were trying to make sense of the moment. The years melted away as they stood there, absorbing the weight of the reunion. It was a bittersweet encounter—one filled with memories of love, loss, and the undeniable bond they once shared. They stood in the middle of the market, surrounded by the lively chaos, yet it felt like they were in their own world, where time had no meaning.

Meera introduced him to her husband, who extended a hand in greeting, embodying warmth and kindness. "It's nice to meet you," he said genuinely, sensing the emotional current between the two. Rahul managed a smile, feeling both admiration and jealousy. He couldn't help but notice the way Meera's eyes sparkled as she spoke to her husband, further deepening his internal conflict.

As they exchanged pleasantries, the conversation felt like a delicate dance, navigating the intricacies of their shared past while acknowledging the present. Rahul's heart swelled with longing and sorrow; he was reminded of all the moments that had led them to this point. Meera was happy, but at what cost?

Despite the tension in the air, they found themselves slipping into comfortable conversation, reminiscing about old times, shared friends, and the adventures they had embarked on together. The ease of their connection was palpable, yet it was layered with an undercurrent of unspoken.

ৡৡৡ

"True success is found in the relentless pursuit of excellence and the courage to explore the unknown, teaching us that our impact and legacy, rather than external accolades, are the true measures of our achievement."

• 61 •

TEN

REDISCOVERING LOVE

"Great things are done by a series of small things brought together. "
- Vincent Van Gogh

In the weeks that followed their unexpected reunion, Rahul found himself engulfed in a whirlwind of emotions. The encounter with Meera had stirred feelings he thought were long buried, leaving him exhilarated and confused. London, with its vibrant energy and endless possibilities, became both a sanctuary and a prison of memories. As he navigated the bustling streets, the weight of longing clung to him like a persistent fog.

Every corner of the city whispered of shared dreams and plans with Meera. He passed by quaint cafés they had talked about visiting, parks where they had imagined picnics under blooming trees, and bookstores filled with titles they once dreamed of reading side by side. Each reminder felt like a gentle nudge to his heart, urging him to confront the reality of their situation. "The heart has its own reasons that reason knows not," he recalled, thinking of how inexplicable love could be.

Despite the emotional turmoil, Rahul decided to embrace this new chapter. He focused on his photography, capturing the essence of life around him while simultaneously documenting his journey of self-discovery. Through his lens, he sought beauty in the everyday—the laughter of children in the park, the vibrant colors of street art, and the quiet moments of reflection. Photography became a therapeutic outlet, helping him process his feelings while keeping him grounded in the present.

As he spent afternoons in the busy streets of Camden, the bustling markets alive with color and sound, he often found himself framing moments that mirrored his emotions. One day, he captured an elderly man feeding pigeons in front of a lively café. The man's weathered hands trembled slightly as he scattered crumbs, and in that moment, Rahul felt a connection to the transient nature of happiness. It was a poignant reminder of how fleeting joy could be, much like his own memories with Meera.

Yet, as days turned into weeks, thoughts of Meera loomed large in his mind. Their brief coffee encounter replayed itself like a favorite film, and he felt a deep desire to connect with her again. He hesitated, though, uncertain about the implications of reaching out. Could they reclaim the friendship that had once been so vital to them, or was it too late? The uncertainty hung in the air, thick and suffocating, like a gray cloud waiting to burst.

One evening, as he reviewed the photos he had taken throughout the week, an image caught his eye. It was a candid shot of Meera's laughter from their last meeting—a moment frozen in time, filled with warmth and light. The moment felt alive in the frame, and he realized he had been living in the shadows of his past, unable to move forward. Inspired by this realization, Rahul made a decision: he would reach out to her.

With a mix of nervousness and excitement, he crafted a message. It was simple yet heartfelt, expressing his desire to meet again and continue their conversation. "The best part of life is the connection we share with others," he reminded himself as he pressed send, his heart racing at the prospect of what might come next.

To his delight, Meera responded quickly, her enthusiasm palpable through the screen. They arranged to meet at a cozy café in the heart of London, known for its artisanal coffee and warm atmosphere. Rahul spent the next few days in a state of anticipation, looking forward to reconnecting with the woman who had once been the center of his universe.

On the day of their meeting, he arrived early, his heart pounding in his chest. The café buzzed with life, the rich aroma of freshly brewed coffee mingling with the sound of laughter and conversation. He chose a quiet corner, a spot where they could talk without distractions, and waited, fidgeting with his camera strap, trying to quell his excitement.

When Meera arrived, the moment felt electric. She walked in, her smile lighting up the room as she spotted him. The warmth of her presence was both comforting and thrilling. They greeted each other with genuine smiles, and Rahul felt as though the years apart had vanished in an instant. "Time can bend, but it never truly breaks the ties that bind us," he thought, feeling the gravity of the moment.

"Thanks for meeting me," Rahul said, his voice filled with a mix of excitement and nervousness.

"I wouldn't miss it for the world," Meera replied, her eyes sparkling with curiosity. They settled into their seats, and the conversation flowed effortlessly, as if no time had passed. They reminisced about their college days, shared stories of their journeys since then, and laughed over the little quirks of life in London.

"Remember that time we got lost trying to find that Indian restaurant?" Rahul chuckled, recalling the hilariously wrong directions they had followed.

"Yes!" Meera laughed, her eyes dancing. "And we ended up at that awful diner instead!"

As they talked, the connection they had once shared began to resurface, rekindling the bond that had always existed beneath the surface. Rahul found himself opening up about his struggles since their separation—the loneliness, the missed opportunities, and the hope he was beginning to find in his new life.

Meera listened intently, her compassion evident in her expression. "I'm so sorry for everything you went through," she said softly. "It's hard to believe how much has happened since then."

"I know," Rahul replied, his heart swelling with gratitude. "But seeing you again has made me realize that I can still find joy. You've always been an important part of my life, Meera."

Their eyes met, and in that moment, a silent understanding passed between them. There was a shared history, a love that had been tested but never truly extinguished. It was as if they both recognized that their feelings had been reignited, but the weight of their current circumstances loomed over them.

"Can I show you something?" Rahul asked suddenly, eager to share his recent work. He pulled out his phone and opened a gallery filled with photos of London—the vibrant streets, serene parks, and candid moments he had captured. As he shared the stories behind each image, he felt a renewed sense of purpose.

Meera watched with admiration, her eyes lighting up at each photograph. "These are incredible, Rahul! You have such a talent for capturing emotion," she said, her voice filled with sincerity.

Encouraged by her praise, he felt a rush of inspiration. "I want to keep creating and exploring," he confessed. "And I'd love to have you by my side, even if just as friends."

The suggestion hung in the air, and Meera smiled, her expression contemplative. "I'd love that, Rahul. I've missed our friendship so much."

As they continued to talk, the atmosphere shifted, growing deeper and more introspective. They began to discuss their feelings, the challenges they faced in their respective lives, and the impact of their past relationship.

Rahul felt a sense of relief in sharing his vulnerability. He explained how he had struggled to cope with the loss of their love, but also how their reunion had sparked a glimmer of hope in him. "You were such a big part of my life," he admitted. "I don't want to lose you again, no matter what form our relationship takes."

Meera nodded, her eyes glistening with understanding. "I feel the same way, Rahul. It's strange how life takes us on different paths, but the connection we had remains. Maybe we can find a way to navigate this new dynamic together."

The conversation deepened, and they found themselves discussing their dreams for the future. Meera shared her aspirations and the challenges of balancing her life with her husband. Rahul listened intently, offering support and encouragement as she navigated her own journey.

As the sun began to set, casting a warm glow through the café windows, Rahul felt a sense of peace enveloping him. He realized that despite the complexities of their past, they had the potential to forge a new path—one that honored their history while embracing the possibilities of the future.

"Perhaps love is not about what you expect to receive, but what you are willing to give," he reflected, understanding that their journey would require patience and openness.

As they parted ways that evening, a mix of emotions enveloped Rahul. He felt lighter than he had in months. The spark between them had been reignited, and he couldn't help but wonder if this was the beginning of a new chapter—a chance to rediscover love in a way that transcended their past.

Days turned into weeks, and the rhythm of their renewed friendship settled into a comforting cadence. They explored London together, visiting art galleries and attending local exhibitions, each experience a thread weaving their lives back together. Rahul marveled at how Meera's laughter filled the spaces around them, making even the grayest days seem brighter.

One Saturday, they found themselves in Hyde Park, surrounded by vibrant autumn leaves that painted the landscape in hues of gold and crimson. They settled on a bench, a gentle breeze stirring the air, and watched families enjoying the day. The serenity of the moment enveloped them.

"This place is magical," Meera said, gazing at the people around them. "I always dreamed of coming here."

"Now you are here," Rahul replied, feeling a warmth spread in his chest. "And you have every right to dream bigger."

As they shared their hopes and aspirations, he felt a renewed sense of purpose blooming within him. "In the midst of movement and chaos, keep stillness inside of you," he recalled, grateful for the tranquility this moment provided.

Their friendship deepened, the unspoken words of affection weaving through their interactions. Rahul cherished every moment, recognizing the beauty in their connection, even if it was complicated. He had learned to appreciate the layers of love, understanding that it could manifest in various forms.

One rainy afternoon, as they huddled in a cozy café, the sound of raindrops tapping against the window created a soothing backdrop for their conversation. The ambiance was filled with the scent of coffee and pastries, a haven from the storm outside.

"Do you remember that day we got caught in the rain?" Rahul asked, a grin spreading across his face. "We ran for shelter and ended up sharing an umbrella."

Meera laughed, her eyes sparkling with memories. "Yes! We were soaked, but it was one of the best days ever."

"Sometimes the unexpected moments create the best memories," he mused, realizing how true that sentiment had become. "Love is not about possession. Love is about appreciation."

Their shared laughter echoed in the small café, and for a moment, it felt as though they were the only two people in the world. The line between friendship and something deeper blurred, and they navigated this new dynamic with tentative steps, each one filled with hope and hesitation.

As autumn gave way to winter, the first snowflakes began to fall over London, transforming the city into a wonderland. Rahul and Meera bundled up and ventured out, exploring the Christmas markets that sprang up across the city. The air was filled with the smell of roasted chestnuts and mulled wine, and the atmosphere buzzed with excitement.

"Let's take a photo!" Meera exclaimed, her cheeks flushed from the cold. They stood in front of a brightly lit Christmas tree, and as Rahul captured the moment, he realized how precious it was to witness her joy. "Life is like a camera. Focus on what's important, capture the good times, and if things don't work out, just take another shot," he reminded himself, feeling inspired.

With each passing day, their friendship grew stronger. Yet, in the quiet moments, Rahul couldn't shake the lingering feelings that danced beneath the surface. The memory of their shared past, the love they once had, tugged at his heart. He began to wonder if they could ever reclaim that intimacy without crossing the fragile line between friendship and romance.

One evening, as they strolled along the Thames, the city lights reflecting on the water's surface, Rahul felt a sense of urgency building within him. He could no longer ignore the feelings that had been bubbling beneath the surface. The time had come to confront the unspoken emotions that lingered between them.

"Meera," he began, his heart racing. "I've been thinking a lot about us… about what we had and what we could have again."

She turned to him, her expression a mix of surprise and curiosity. "What do you mean?"

"I know we've been navigating this friendship carefully, but I can't help but feel that there's something more here," he confessed, his voice steady despite the turmoil within. "You've been an integral part of my life, and I can't deny that my feelings for you have grown stronger."

The world around them faded into the background as Meera absorbed his words. For a moment, silence enveloped them, heavy with the weight of possibility. Rahul held his breath, waiting for her response.

"Rahul, I've felt it too," she finally said, her voice soft but filled with conviction. "But I didn't know how to bring it up. There's so much at stake."

"I understand," he replied, his heart aching with vulnerability. "But I believe that we can navigate this together. Life is too short to let fear hold us back from what truly matters."

They stood there, two souls intertwined in the quiet of the night, the moonlight illuminating their faces. In that moment, Rahul realized that love was not merely about possession; it was about choice, about embracing the complexities of each other's lives.

"We may not have control over everything, but we can choose how we respond," he said softly, a sense of clarity washing over him.

Meera smiled, a radiant expression that lit up her face. "I want to explore this with you, Rahul. I've missed you so much."

As they walked hand in hand along the river, Rahul felt a profound sense of hope. This was not just a rekindling of a past love; it was the beginning of something new, something that honored their journey while embracing the possibilities ahead.

With every step they took, Rahul felt the weight of the past lift, replaced by the promise of a future filled with laughter, understanding, and love. The spark between them had reignited, and he couldn't help but believe that this was the beginning of a beautiful journey—a chance to rediscover love in a way that transcended their past.

ppp

"Embracing your unique journey, fostering collaboration, and empowering others to shine are foundational to creating meaningful impact and achieving personal growth."

ELEVEN

EMBRACING THE PAST

"Nostalgia is a file that removes the rough edges from the good old days"
- Doug Larson

As the weeks rolled into months, Rahul and Meera's connection deepened amidst the vibrant streets of London. Each day felt like a page in a story they were both eager to write, filled with moments that shimmered like the city lights. With every coffee date, gallery visit, and leisurely stroll through the city's lush parks, they began to embrace the complexities of their past while forging a new path forward.

The city, alive with culture and diversity, mirrored their journey—a blend of nostalgia and hope, joy and pain. Rahul often found himself marveling at the changes in Meera. She was no longer the same girl he had fallen in love with years ago; she was more resilient, shaped by the trials she had faced. Her laughter still held the same warmth, but there was a maturity in her eyes, a wisdom that came from life's experiences. He admired how she navigated her life with grace, balancing the demands of her marriage with her personal aspirations.

One brisk afternoon, they found themselves at the iconic British Museum, surrounded by centuries of history. The grandeur of the architecture inspired them, and they wandered through exhibits, fingers brushing against ancient artifacts. "Can you imagine the stories these objects could tell?" Rahul mused, gazing at a collection of Greek vases.

"Every artifact is a reminder that history lives on," Meera replied, her eyes shining. "Just like our own stories."

During their outings, they explored iconic landmarks, art exhibitions, and hidden gems scattered throughout the city. Each shared moment was laced with laughter and deep conversation, allowing them to peel back the layers of their past. They spoke candidly about their experiences since their separation, each story revealing a piece of their hearts.

One day, while exploring the colorful streets of Camden Market, surrounded by an array of eclectic shops and vibrant street art, they paused to sit on a bench near the canal. The atmosphere buzzed with creativity, and Rahul felt inspired. "This place feels alive," he said, taking in the energy around them. "It reminds me of how we used to dream about exploring the world together."

Meera smiled, her eyes sparkling. "We had so many plans, didn't we? It's strange how life took us on such different paths. But I'm glad we're here now." Her voice held a wistful tone, and he realized that both of them had harbored dreams unfulfilled.

"Life has a way of shaping our journeys," he replied thoughtfully. "Perhaps we're meant to find each other again at this moment."

Their conversation shifted to the memories they cherished—the late-night study sessions, the spontaneous adventures, and the laughter that had once filled their days. They reminisced about the small things: the way Meera would always sneak snacks into the library or how Rahul would tease her about her obsession with romantic novels. Each memory felt like a thread weaving their shared history, binding them closer together. Yet he couldn't shake the feeling of something unfinished, a part of their story left untold.

Yet amidst the warmth of their connection, there were still unaddressed wounds. They both understood that their journey was not just about rediscovering love but also about healing the scars left by their separation. One evening, as they shared a quiet moment in a cozy café, Rahul sensed the weight of unsaid words hanging in the air.

"Meera," he began, his voice steady but vulnerable, "there's something I've been meaning to talk about. The way things ended between us... it still weighs on my heart. I never wanted to hurt you, and I've often wondered if we could have done things differently."

Meera's expression softened, and she nodded, her eyes reflecting understanding. "I've thought about it too, Rahul. The circumstances were beyond our control. We were young, and there were so many pressures. It wasn't just our love that was tested—it was everything around us." He felt the knot in his chest loosen slightly; honesty had a way of making burdens feel lighter.

"Sometimes we must walk through the shadows to find our light," he said softly, hoping to express the complex emotions that lingered in the air.

Their conversation delved into the painful moments of their past—the misunderstandings, the influence of family, and the pressures they faced. They spoke of the hurt and confusion that had led to their breakup, and in doing so, they began to dismantle the walls they had built around their hearts.

"I want you to know," Meera said softly, "that I've learned a lot since then. I've realized that love isn't just about the beautiful moments; it's also about facing challenges together. I wish we could have done that."

Rahul's heart ached at her words, but he felt a sense of relief in their honesty. "I wish that too. I've carried the weight of our separation for so long. It's been hard to let go, knowing we never really had closure." A surge of hope welled within him; perhaps this conversation would be the first step toward healing.

The acknowledgment of their pain created a space for healing. They recognized that while the past could not be changed, they had the power to redefine their relationship moving forward. Together, they made a pact to embrace their shared history, to learn from it, and to navigate their feelings with openness and authenticity.

In the weeks that followed, they engaged in deeper discussions, exploring their hopes and fears. Rahul learned more about Meera's experiences since their breakup—how she had navigated her marriage, the challenges she faced, and the moments of joy she had found along the way. She spoke of her husband's kindness, acknowledging the support he provided, but also the complexities that came with it. He couldn't help but feel a twinge of jealousy, but he quickly suppressed it; he knew they were in different places now.

One chilly evening, as they walked through the streets of Southbank adorned with twinkling fairy lights, Meera stopped to admire a street performer. "It's amazing how art brings people together," she said, her eyes reflecting the lights. "It's like we're all connected through our stories, isn't it?"

"Absolutely," Rahul replied, his heart swelling with affection. "Every artist is a storyteller, weaving emotions into their craft. Just like we're weaving our own story now."

In turn, Rahul shared his own struggles—the isolation he had felt, the guilt over their past, and the desire to create a meaningful life in London. He spoke about his passion for photography, how it had become a way to express himself and connect with the world around him.

"Photography allows me to capture fleeting moments," he explained, showing her a series of photographs on his phone. "Each click is a reminder that beauty exists, even in the ordinary."

Meera scrolled through the images, her eyes lighting up with admiration. "You have a gift, Rahul. You capture emotion so beautifully. It's like you see the world through a different lens." He felt a sense of pride swell within him, knowing that she understood him in a way that few others did.

As they delved into their vulnerabilities, they found themselves growing closer. They began to forge a friendship rooted in understanding and compassion, allowing the remnants of their romantic feelings to coexist with the new bond they were building.

One evening, while walking along the Thames, the city illuminated by twinkling lights, Meera paused to take in the view.

"This city feels like a fresh start for both of us," she said, her voice filled with hope. "I'm grateful we can explore it together."

Rahul looked at her, his heart swelling with affection. "I never imagined I would have the chance to reconnect with you like this. It feels like we're writing a new story, one that honors our past but also opens the door to new possibilities."

"As we move forward, let's not forget the lessons we've learned," Meera said, her gaze steady. "The past can shape us, but it doesn't have to define our future."

As they continued their walk, they felt the weight of the past lifting. The shared experiences they had navigated together became the foundation for a renewed connection. They were both older and wiser, ready to embrace the complexities of love and friendship without the fear of what had come before.

"Do you ever think about what could have been?" Meera asked, her tone contemplative.

"Sometimes," Rahul replied, his gaze fixed on the shimmering water. "But I believe that everything we went through was necessary for us to grow. The universe has a way of guiding us to where we need to be." He thought of the serendipity that had brought them together again, how life often led them down unexpected paths that were ultimately for their benefit.

In that moment, standing by the river with the city as their backdrop, they made a silent promise to support each other in whatever path lay ahead. They understood that love is not simply about possession or timing; it's about being there for one another, navigating life's uncertainties, and cherishing the bond they had rekindled.

As the stars began to twinkle in the night sky, Rahul felt a sense of peace settle within him. He realized that while their past would always be a part of them, it didn't have to define their future. Together, they could embrace the journey, open to love in all its forms—friendship, partnership, and perhaps something even deeper.

One brisk morning, they decided to visit the historic Tower of London. The air was crisp, and the early sunlight cast a golden hue over the ancient stones. As they explored the fortress, Rahul felt a surge of excitement, both for the history surrounding them and for the memories they were creating together.

"This place has seen so much," he remarked, gazing at the medieval architecture. "It's a reminder that even the strongest structures can weather storms."

Meera nodded, her expression thoughtful. "Just like relationships. They require strength, resilience, and the willingness to adapt." She paused, and he sensed she was about to share something deeper.

Later, as they stood before the Crown Jewels, Meera marveled at the opulence. "These treasures are beautiful, but I think the true gems in life are the moments we share," she said, her eyes shining.

"Exactly," Rahul replied, feeling the weight of her words. "Moments can be far more valuable than anything material." The realization hung in the air between them, a shared understanding of the importance of connection over possessions.

As the sun dipped below the horizon, painting the sky in hues of orange and pink, Rahul felt a sense of gratitude wash over him. He realized that life was not about holding onto what had been lost but about embracing the possibilities of what could be. And as he glanced at Meera, her face illuminated by the warm glow of the setting sun, he knew that they were just beginning to write the next chapter of their lives together—one filled with promise, growth, and perhaps a love that had been reborn.

ϷϷϷ

"The essence of true growth lies not in the external validation we seek from those we love but in the internal validation we cultivate within ourselves. Our worth is not measured by another's ability to recognize it, nor is our journey's significance diminished by their inability to walk it with us."

TWELVE
A LOVE TRANSCENDED

"Love does not live on the lips of those who speak love but in the heart of those who are truly in love. "
-Anonymous

As the months slipped by, the connection between Rahul and Meera transformed into something more profound than either could have anticipated. Their initial reunion had ignited a spark, an excitement that buzzed in the air, but as the days turned into weeks, that spark blossomed into a warm, abiding friendship. It was rooted in mutual respect and a deep understanding, yet beneath the surface of their camaraderie, old feelings stirred, whispering their timeless truths, lingering like soft shadows in the corners of their hearts.

London, with its vibrant streets and endless energy, provided the perfect backdrop for this renewed bond. The city was alive, teeming with culture and life, and it echoed their own journey of rediscovery. They meandered through art galleries where every painting told a story, attended music festivals where the notes danced like fireflies in the summer night, and shared quiet moments in serene parks, their laughter weaving through the crisp autumn air like threads of golden sunlight.

One particularly beautiful afternoon, they found themselves wandering through Kew Gardens, a haven of tranquility amidst the urban chaos. Surrounded by a kaleidoscope of vibrant flowers and towering trees that whispered secrets in the gentle breeze, Meera paused, her breath caught by the beauty around her. "You know, this place feels magical," she said, her eyes sparkling with delight, reflecting the colors of the blooms around them. "It's like nature is reminding us that life is ever-changing, yet beautiful in its complexity."

Rahul smiled, captivated not only by the landscape but by her perspective on life. "It really is. Just like our lives, right? We've faced challenges, yet here we are, finding beauty in our journey."

As they wandered deeper into the garden, they stumbled upon a secluded spot by a tranquil pond, the sunlight filtering through the leaves like liquid gold. Sitting on a weathered bench, they were cocooned in a moment of serenity, their hearts in sync as they shared their hopes for the future. Each word spoken was a delicate brushstroke on the canvas of their relationship, painting a picture of dreams intertwined.

Meera spoke passionately about her aspirations to pursue art, her creativity reigniting after years of neglect. "I've always wanted to paint the stories I see around me," she confided, her voice tinged with a mix of hope and hesitation. "But I've let fear and doubt hold me back."

"Your art has always inspired me," Rahul said sincerely, his gaze steady. "You have a gift, and you deserve to share it with the world. Don't let anything dim your light."

Encouraged by his words, Meera felt a spark of courage blossom within her. Their conversation deepened, taking on an intimate tone as they began to explore their feelings. A hush enveloped them, punctuated only by the rustle of leaves and the soft chirping of birds. "Rahul, I've been thinking a lot about us," she began, her heart racing with the weight of her confession. "It's been such a long time since we've been together, and yet... I feel like the connection we have is still there, even stronger than before."

The air between them was charged with emotion, a palpable current that drew them closer. Rahul's breath caught in his throat. He had felt it too—the way their chemistry crackled in the air, the unspoken bond that pulled them together like gravity. "I know what you mean," he admitted, his voice barely above a whisper. "It's like we're different people now, shaped by our experiences, yet that love is still a part of us. I can't deny how much I care for you."

In that moment, the world outside the garden faded, leaving just the two of them, caught in a web of vulnerability and longing. Meera's heart raced as she considered the implications of their feelings. "But what about my marriage?" she asked softly, her voice trembling with uncertainty. "I don't want to hurt anyone."

Rahul nodded, understanding the weight of her words. "I respect that. It's important to consider the impact of our choices. But I also believe that we owe it to ourselves to explore what we have together. It feels too significant to ignore."

Meera took a deep breath, feeling the gravity of the moment settle around them like a heavy fog. "You're right. We've been given this second chance, and I don't want to waste it. But we need to be honest about what this means for both of us and for my husband."

With the sunlight casting a warm glow over them, they made a pact to approach their feelings with care and transparency. They agreed to communicate openly, to explore their connection while remaining respectful of the lives they had built. It was a delicate balance, yet both felt a renewed sense of purpose in navigating it together.

In the weeks that followed, they took their time, savoring each moment, letting their feelings deepen naturally. They began to peel back the layers of their past, confronting fears and insecurities that had once kept them apart. Each shared story was a step towards healing, a bridge over the chasm of time that had separated them.

One chilly evening, wrapped in scarves and jackets, they found themselves in a quaint café, steam rising from their mugs of hot chocolate. Rahul shared his struggles with loneliness, the impact of their separation weighing heavily on his heart. "I felt lost without you," he confessed, his voice steady but tinged with vulnerability. "Every day felt like I was carrying this invisible weight."

Meera listened intently, grateful for his honesty, her heart aching for the pain he had endured. "I didn't know," she whispered. "I was so caught up in my own struggles that I never considered how you felt. I've felt torn between family expectations and my own desires, and the guilt of how we ended left scars I'm still healing from."

Their vulnerability fostered an environment of trust, allowing them to explore the possibility of a romantic relationship while being mindful of Meera's marriage. They both understood that their bond was rare, and they wanted to nurture it without causing further pain.

As they continued to meet, Meera began to have open conversations with her husband about her feelings and the changes she was experiencing. "I need to be honest with you," she said one evening, her heart pounding as she broached the subject. "I've reconnected with Rahul, and it's stirred feelings I thought I had buried."

Her husband, a kind and understanding man, listened attentively as she poured out her heart. They spoke honestly about the complexities of their relationship, allowing space for both love and uncertainty. Over time, he came to understand that love can be multifaceted, recognizing the importance of Meera exploring her feelings with Rahul.

"It's difficult, but I want you to be happy," he said softly, the warmth in his voice belying the weight of their conversation. "If exploring this connection with Rahul is what you need, then you have my support."

Meanwhile, Rahul immersed himself in his photography, capturing moments of beauty that mirrored his journey with Meera. Each click of the shutter was a release, a way to pour his emotions into something tangible. He sought out the light in everyday scenes—the way the sun filtered through the trees, casting playful shadows, the laughter of children in the park, the quiet moments of reflection that often went unnoticed.

As the seasons changed in London, so too did their relationship. The initial thrill of rekindled love evolved into a deeper understanding, one that transcended the confines of their past. They began to envision what life could look like if they fully embraced their feelings. It was a daunting yet exhilarating prospect, the promise of what lay ahead glimmering like stars in a night sky.

One evening, as they stood on the banks of the Thames, watching the sunset paint the sky in hues of orange and pink, Rahul turned to Meera, his heart brimming with emotion. "I believe in us," he said, his voice steady and sincere, cutting through the silence like a lifeline. "Whatever the future holds, I want to face it together. You mean too much to me to walk away."

Meera felt a surge of warmth at his words, like a gentle tide washing over her worries. "I feel the same way, Rahul. We've come so far, and I don't want to lose what we have again. We deserve a chance to find our way back to each other."

In that moment, surrounded by the beauty of the city they had come to love, they shared a quiet promise—one that acknowledged their past but looked forward to the future. Their love, once interrupted, was now poised to transcend the boundaries that had once separated them.

"Love is not about possession," Meera mused, her voice a soft whisper. "It's about appreciation and respect. It's about allowing the other person to grow."

Rahul nodded, his gaze unwavering. "And sometimes, love means making difficult choices, even if it hurts. It's a journey of discovery, not just of the other person, but of ourselves."

With open hearts and a commitment to embrace whatever came next, Rahul and Meera stepped forward together, ready to face the complexities of love, friendship, and the potential of a shared future. The journey ahead would not be without its challenges, but they were determined to navigate it hand in hand, their love a beacon guiding them through the uncertainties of life.

As the evening turned to night and the stars began to twinkle above, they stood side by side, watching the river flow, each ripple a reminder of their own journey—twisting, turning, but ultimately moving forward, together.

ᗘᗘᗘ

"The true essence of love lies not in its reciprocation, but in the depth of our feelings and the courage to express them. Loving in its purest form stands as a testament to our personal growth and a pathway to inner peace."

THIRTEEN

BUILDING A FUTURE

"Life is a journey, not a destination. "
- Ralph Waldo Emerson

As the spring sun began to warm the streets of London, Rahul and Meera found themselves in a newfound rhythm. Their bond, strengthened by months of exploration and honest conversations, now pulsed with the promise of a shared future. Each passing day, they wove their lives together, blending their aspirations, fears, and dreams into a tapestry that reflected both their individuality and their connection. The vibrant life around them mirrored the blossoming of their relationship; the cherry blossoms floated in the breeze like whispered promises of new beginnings.

Their conversations grew deeper, spanning everything from mundane day-to-day experiences to the profound hopes they held for the future. One evening, they sat on a park bench in Hyde Park, the golden hour casting a warm glow around them. "You know," Meera began, gazing at the sun dipping below the horizon, "I've always believed that art has a way of capturing the beauty of fleeting moments." She turned to Rahul, her eyes shining. "Just like this moment. It feels so perfect."

Rahul smiled, feeling the warmth of her gaze wrap around him like a soft blanket. "It is perfect, and I think you have that same ability in your art—to encapsulate emotions and experiences. Your paintings breathe life."

Encouraged by his words, Meera felt a rush of inspiration. "I want to create something that resonates with others, something that speaks to the heart. I want my work to inspire people to embrace their own journeys."

As spring danced its way into summer, Meera dedicated herself to her art. She enrolled in classes that reignited her creativity, challenging herself to experiment with different styles and mediums. Rahul supported her wholeheartedly, often accompanying her to galleries or helping her set up for exhibitions. He captured her artistic journey through his photography, celebrating her talent and determination.

One weekend, while wandering through a local art fair, Meera spotted a booth showcasing an opportunity for emerging artists to display their work in a collective exhibition. Her heart raced with excitement, but doubt crept in. "What if no one likes my work?" she worried aloud, biting her lip.

Rahul took her hand, his gaze steady and encouraging. "You have an incredible gift, Meera. Your art speaks volumes. This is your chance to show it to the world. I believe in you." His support infused her with courage, and after a moment's hesitation, she decided to submit her pieces.

As the days turned into weeks, Meera poured her heart into her art, often losing herself in the colors and canvases that reflected her innermost feelings. Each brushstroke was a reflection of her journey—of love, loss, and rediscovery. Rahul was her biggest cheerleader, attending every session, bringing her coffee, and providing thoughtful feedback. Their shared moments in the studio were filled with laughter, creativity, and the warmth of their deepening connection.

However, amidst their excitement, Meera also faced the reality of her marriage. Her conversations with her husband continued, rooted in honesty and respect. She made it clear that while she cherished their time together, she needed the freedom to explore her feelings for Rahul. They both agreed that it was essential to navigate this transition thoughtfully, prioritizing open communication.

One evening, as the sun began to set, casting a golden hue over their cozy living room, Meera's husband sat across from her, his expression serious but compassionate. "I appreciate your honesty, Meera. I can see how much this means to you." He took a deep breath. "But it's not easy for me. I don't want to lose you, but I also don't want to hold you back from your happiness."

Meera's heart ached at the thought of hurting him. "I want you to know that I value everything we've built together. You've been my anchor through so much. But I also need to explore who I am outside of this marriage, to follow my passions without feeling confined."

He nodded slowly, understanding the complexity of their situation. "I just want you to be happy. If that means exploring things with Rahul, then I can accept that, even if it's difficult for me." His eyes held a mix of sadness and acceptance.

Meanwhile, Rahul was experiencing a resurgence in his own life. His photography business began to flourish as he gained recognition for his work. He took on projects that allowed him to blend his artistic vision with meaningful storytelling, often reflecting the emotions of love, loss, and resilience. The success reinvigorated him, reminding him that he could pursue his passions alongside his connection with Meera.

One afternoon, while wandering through a quaint neighborhood in East London, Rahul and Meera stumbled upon a charming little café with outdoor seating. It had an inviting atmosphere, filled with the aroma of freshly brewed coffee and baked goods. They settled at a table under the shade of a blooming cherry blossom tree, enjoying the gentle breeze.

As they sipped their drinks, Meera spoke of her upcoming exhibition, her excitement palpable. "I can't believe it's finally happening. This is a huge step for me," she said, her eyes shining.

"I can't wait to see your work displayed," Rahul replied, his voice filled with pride. "You've put your heart and soul into this, and it deserves to be celebrated."

Their conversation drifted toward future dreams, with Meera expressing her desire to create a space for artists—a gallery that would foster creativity and community. Rahul's eyes lit up at the idea. "That sounds incredible! We could work on it together," he suggested, envisioning a collaborative effort that blended their talents.

Meera beamed at the thought. "Would you really want to? It could be a place where artists can share their work and find support, just like we've found in each other."

"Absolutely," Rahul affirmed, his excitement matching hers. "We could organize workshops, host exhibitions, and create a community that nurtures creativity. It's a beautiful vision."

With their ambitions aligned, they began to sketch out plans for the gallery, mapping out ideas and envisioning how they could bring their dreams to life. Their discussions were filled with enthusiasm, laughter, and a sense of purpose, as they realized they were not just building a future for themselves but also a shared legacy.

As the exhibition day approached, Meera's nerves began to build. The night before, they found themselves in the cozy warmth of Rahul's apartment, surrounded by her artwork. Meera paced the room, anxiety bubbling within her. "What if no one shows up? What if my work doesn't resonate?"

Rahul stepped forward, gently placing his hands on her shoulders. "Meera, this is about more than just the exhibition. It's about you expressing yourself and taking a step towards your dreams. You've already accomplished so much. Trust in your talent."

His words anchored her, grounding her in the moment. They spent the evening preparing, laughing and reminiscing about their journey together. Rahul took candid photographs of Meera with her art, capturing the essence of her creativity and the love they shared.

Finally, the day of the exhibition arrived. The gallery buzzed with energy as artists and art enthusiasts filled the space. Meera stood nervously by her pieces, but Rahul was by her side, providing unwavering support. As guests began to engage with her work, she felt a wave of validation wash over her.

One by one, people approached her, sharing their thoughts and interpretations. Meera's heart swelled with pride, knowing her art was resonating with others. Rahul watched her blossom, captivated by her passion and grace.

As the evening unfolded, he felt a sense of fulfillment, witnessing the woman he loved step into her power. Their shared dream was coming to life, a beautiful manifestation of their journey together.

Later that night, as the event drew to a close, Meera found Rahul in a quiet corner of the gallery. "Thank you for believing in me," she said, her eyes glistening with gratitude. "I couldn't have done this without you."

He smiled, warmth radiating from his heart. "You did this all on your own, Meera. I just had the privilege of standing beside you."

In that moment, surrounded by the remnants of the evening's success, they shared a kiss—a tender, lingering promise that they would continue to support and uplift each other as they built their future together.

From that day forward, their lives intertwined in beautiful ways. They collaborated on the gallery, hosted events, and nurtured a community of artists. The journey was filled with challenges, but they faced each obstacle hand in hand, their love and partnership growing stronger with every step.

As they built their life together, they learned the importance of balance—between ambition and love, dreams and reality. Their relationship was a testament to the resilience of the human spirit, a reminder that true love can endure and flourish, even amidst life's complexities.

The Beautiful Ending

With each passing day, Rahul and Meera continued to create a future filled with hope, laughter, and endless possibilities. Together, they embraced the journey, knowing that they had finally found their way back to each other—proving that love, once transcended, can become a powerful force for growth and transformation.

Seasons changed, painting the canvas of London in vibrant colors, much like the palette of Meera's artwork. The cherry blossoms bloomed anew each spring, serving as a reminder of their resilience. Their gallery became a sanctuary for artists, a place where creativity thrived, friendships blossomed, and dreams took flight.

One evening, as they closed the gallery for the night, Rahul turned to Meera, his heart full of gratitude. "Can you believe how far we've come? From two people searching for their paths to this beautiful life we've built together."

Meera smiled, the warmth of their shared history enveloping her. "It's like we've painted our own masterpiece, filled with vibrant strokes of love and adventure."

"Life truly is an art," Rahul said, taking her hand in his. "And every day, we get to create our own story."

In that moment, they stood together, watching the city lights twinkle like stars against the canvas of the night sky. They had learned that love was not just a feeling but an art form itself—one that required vulnerability, trust, and a willingness to embrace the unknown.

As they walked hand in hand through the streets of London, they felt an overwhelming sense of gratitude for the journey that had brought them together. "To love," Meera whispered, her voice filled with emotion.

"To love," Rahul echoed, pulling her close. "To the beauty of our journey and the future we will continue to create together."

And so, they stepped into their tomorrow, hearts intertwined, ready to face whatever came their way. For in their love, they had found not only each other but the courage to build a life that celebrated both their individuality and their union. With each step they took, they embraced the unfolding of their story—a narrative rich with hope, creativity, and the everlasting magic of love.

 app

"*When our minds are overwhelmed by passion and turmoil, the journey toward inner peace and happiness frequently leads us through the realm of spirituality. Defined in its essence, spirituality is the pursuit of purpose, meaning, and connection in our lives. It invites us to venture beyond the tangible, material world to seek the profound truths that lie within ourselves and the universe at large. This pursuit might encompass religious beliefs, personal introspection, meditation, or a deep connection with the natural world, all with the aim of nurturing a state of tranquility and well being.*"

"Thousands of candles can be lit from a single candle, and the life of the candle will not be shortened. Happiness never decreases by being shared. "
Attributed to Budha

A Love That Endures

"The best and most beautiful things in the world cannot be seen or even touched - they must be felt with the heart. "
- Helen Keller

Years had passed since Rahul and Meera first walked hand in hand along the vibrant streets of London, their lives intertwined in ways they had never anticipated. The city had become a canvas for their love story, a backdrop to their trials and triumphs. Now, as they strolled along the banks of the Thames, the setting sun casting a warm golden hue over the water, they found themselves reflecting on the extraordinary journey that had led them to this moment.

The river flowed steadily beside them, a reminder of the passage of time. Each ripple seemed to echo the challenges they had faced—the heartache, the misunderstandings, and the moments of doubt. Yet, through it all, their love had remained a constant, a guiding light that illuminated even the darkest of days.

"Can you believe how far we've come?" Meera said, her voice soft yet filled with wonder. She paused to admire the view—the iconic skyline, the shimmering water, and the people bustling about, all contributing to the vibrant life around them. "It feels like a dream."

Rahul smiled, squeezing her hand gently. "It really does. I remember those early days of uncertainty, and now look at us." He glanced at her, his heart swelling with pride. "We built a life together, and it's everything we dreamed of."

Their journey had been filled with moments of joy—like the opening of their gallery, where local artists found a platform to showcase their talents. The space had become a beloved community hub, brimming with creativity and connection. They hosted events that celebrated art, love, and friendship, each gathering a testament to the bond they shared.

But their path had not been without its hurdles. They had faced doubts from friends and family, challenges in balancing their personal and professional lives, and the complexities of navigating a relationship that had once been marred by separation. Yet, each obstacle had only strengthened their resolve, proving that love, when nurtured with understanding and patience, could weather any storm.

"Remember the day of my exhibition?" Meera asked, her eyes sparkling with nostalgia. "I was so nervous, but you were right there beside me, cheering me on."

"Of course," Rahul chuckled, recalling the way she had glowed that night, surrounded by her art. "You were incredible. I knew then that you were destined for greatness."

"And you captured every moment so beautifully," she replied, her expression softening. "Your support has always meant the world to me."

They walked on, reminiscing about the countless memories they had created together—the late-night conversations filled with dreams, the quiet mornings spent sipping coffee, and the laughter that echoed in their home. Each moment had woven a rich tapestry of love, trust, and companionship, one that had transformed them into partners in every sense of the word.

As they reached a scenic overlook, the Thames stretched out before them, sparkling under the evening light. Rahul turned to Meera, a serious yet tender expression on his face. "You know, I've learned that love isn't just about the grand gestures or the perfect moments. It's about being there for each other, especially when times get tough."

Meera nodded, her heart full. "It's the little things, isn't it? The everyday choices we make to support each other, to grow together. That's what makes our love so strong."

In that moment, they understood that their relationship was a continuous journey—a living testament to the power of love. It was not static or defined by a single narrative but rather a dynamic dance of growth, respect, and unwavering support.

As they stood there, watching the sun dip below the horizon, casting a warm glow over the city, they felt a profound sense of gratitude. They had faced adversity and come out stronger, not just as individuals, but as a couple who had chosen each other time and again.

With the promise of tomorrow ahead of them, they turned to leave, hand in hand. Their future was a blank canvas, filled with the potential for new adventures, challenges, and, above all, love.

Together, they looked forward to a lifetime of shared dreams, knowing that as long as they had each other, they could weather any storm. Their hearts brimmed with hope, laughter, and the sweet knowledge that true love, once found, endures through time and trials, flourishing in the warmth of unwavering connection.

And so, with the sun setting behind them, Rahul and Meera walked forward into their shared future—confident, committed, and ready for whatever life had in store. Their love story, rich with history and promise, was far from over; it had only just begun.

ppp

"Every setback, heartbreak, or challenge carries the seed of an equal or greater opportunity. Our task is to nurture that seed, water it with hope, resilience, and purpose."

Share Your Journey

As we reach the close of our journey together through these pages, I hope you've found moments of reflection, inspiration, and perhaps even transformation. While I've shared lessons at the end of each chapter that hold deep meaning to me, I believe that the true power of this journey lies in the unique insights each of us gains along the way.

Your experiences, reflections, and revelations are invaluable, not only to you but to the wider community we're building together through these shared stories. Therefore, I invite you to share your own understanding and takeaways from this book. Did a particular lesson resonate with you? Have you experienced a moment of clarity or transformation inspired by a story or exercise within these pages? Or perhaps you've discovered a personal insight that extends beyond the lessons I've shared.

Whatever your reflections may be, I would be honored to hear from you. You can share your journey with me via email at Shanuchandra2485@gmail.com or direct message me on Instagram. Your stories inspire me, and with your permission, I hope to share them with our growing community to inspire others as well.

This book is not the end but a beginning—a stepping stone into the vast landscape of personal growth and understanding. Let's continue to support and inspire one another as we each walk our unique paths.

With gratitude and anticipation,
Shanu Chandra

About The Author

Shanu Chandra, a B.Tech graduate and accomplished business professional, is driven by a profound passion for writing and self-expression. With a rich background in the business world, Shanu has cultivated a unique perspective on life and relationships, which he passionately shares through his literary endeavors.

His latest work, Echoes of Love, is a heartfelt exploration of human connections and the transformative power of love. Inspired by his personal experiences and observations, Shanu aims to delve into the intricacies of relationships, offering readers insights that resonate on multiple levels. He believes that love, in its many forms, has the potential to heal, inspire, and elevate individuals, guiding them toward a deeper understanding of themselves and those around them.

Beyond his business pursuits, Shanu is committed to fostering meaningful connections and uplifting others through his writing. He views literature as a powerful tool for reflection and growth, inviting readers to embark on a journey of self-discovery and emotional exploration.

Through Echoes of Love, Shanu encourages us to embrace vulnerability and openness, reminding us that within the realm of love lies the capacity for profound change. His narrative not only reflects his philosophy but also serves as a beacon for anyone seeking to navigate the complexities of relationships with grace and authenticity.

www.ingramcontent.com/pod-product-compliance
Lightning Source LLC
Chambersburg PA
CBHW031309130726
47988CB00007B/2776